THE SISTERS GRIMM

2

THE STORY GRID

10th Anniversary Edition

THE UNUSUAL SUSPECTS

MICHAEL BUCKLEY

Pictures by PETER FERGUSON

AMULET BOOKS · NEW YORK

Cataloging-in-Publication Data has been applied for and may be obtained from the Library of Congress.

ISBN: 978-1-4197-2008-6

Text copyright © 2005, 2017 Michael Buckley
Illustrations copyright © 2005 Peter Ferguson
Book design by Siobhán Gallagher

Printed and bound in U.S.A.
10 9 8 7 6

Amulet Books are available at special discounts when purchased in quantity for premiums and promotions as well as fundraising or educational use. Special editions can also be created to specification. For details, contact specialsales@abramsbooks.com or the address below.

ABRAMS The Art of Books
195 Broadway, New York, NY 10007
abramsbooks.com

For the friends who shaped my life: Michael Madonia, Michael Nemeth, Todd Johnson, Ronald Schultz, Ed Kellet, and Heather Averill Farley

Sabrina scrambled through the darkness, armed with only a shovel. She used the cold stone walls as a guide. Each step was a challenge to her balance and senses. She stumbled on jagged rocks and accidentally kicked over an abandoned tool, sending a clanging echo off the tunnel walls. Whatever was waiting for her in the labyrinth knew she was coming now. Yet she couldn't turn back. Her family was somewhere in the twisting maze, and no one else could help them. Sabrina prayed they were still alive.

The tunnel made a sharp turn, and around the corner Sabrina spotted a distant, flickering light. She quickened her pace, and soon the tunnel emptied into an enormous cave carved out of the bedrock of Ferryport Landing. Torches mounted on the walls gave the room a dull light and created dancing black shadows. But aside from a few old buckets and a couple of shovels that leaned against a crumbling wall, Sabrina was completely alone. Another dead end! She had just turned to retrace her steps when something hit her squarely in the back, knocking her to the ground. She fell heavily onto her arm, and the searing pain told her it was broken. She groaned in agony, but her distress was drowned out by an odd clicking and hissing.

She crawled to her feet and grabbed the shovel with her good arm, swinging it around threateningly.

"I've come for my family!" she shouted into the darkness beyond the torchlight. Her voice bounced back at her from all sides of the cave.

Her ears filled with a cold, arrogant chuckle, and a long, spindly leg struck out from the shadows, narrowly missing her head. It slammed against the wall, pulverizing stone into dust. Sabrina swung wildly at the leg, sinking the sharp edge of the shovel into the monster's flesh. Its shrieks were deafening.

"I'm not going to be easy to kill," Sabrina said, hoping her voice sounded more confident to the monster than it did in her own ears.

"Kill you? Don't you understand? This is a party!" a voice replied. "And you're the guest of honor."

1

Three Days Earlier

L ET'S GET THIS PARTY STARTED, ALREADY!"
Sabrina grumbled as she rubbed another cramp out
of her leg. For the last three nights she and her seven-
year-old sister, Daphne, had been crouching behind a stack of
Diaper Rash Donna dolls waiting for criminals to rob Geppetto's
Toyshop. She was tired, hungry, and more than a little irritated.
She should have been at home, sleeping in her own bed, not using
a board game as a pillow.

"Shhh! You'll wake him," Daphne said, pointing to their two-
hundred-pound Great Dane. Elvis was lying next to a display of
yo-yos, sound asleep. Sabrina couldn't help but envy him.

"Girls, you have to be quiet," Granny Relda said as she huddled
behind some foam rubber footballs. "The crooks could come at
any second!"

In most ordinary towns, the police do not rely on two kids and a sleeping dog to solve crimes, but Ferryport Landing was no ordinary town. More than half of its residents were part of a secret community known as Everafters. Everafters were actually fairy-tale characters who had migrated from far and wide to the United States more than two hundred years ago. They had settled in the little town and now used magical disguises to live and work alongside their human neighbors. Ogres worked at the post office, witches ran the twenty-four-hour diner, and the legendary Prince Charming served as the town's mayor. The humans were none the wiser—except the Grimms.

Sabrina would have been happy to live in blissful ignorance, but her family had been involved with Everafters since her great-great-great-great-grandfather Wilhelm Grimm and his brother, Jacob, helped establish Ferryport Landing. Some might think it thrilling to live next door to fairies and princesses, but Sabrina felt like she was trapped inside a bad dream. Most of the Everafters saw her family as their bitter enemies, largely because of the magical curse Wilhelm and a witch named Baba Yaga had used to trap them within the town's borders. It stopped a war between the Everafters and the humans, but it also created an invisible cage. No Everafter could leave Ferryport Landing unless the Grimms abandoned the town or died out. More than a few folks would have been happy to see either happen.

Even with that dark cloud hanging over her family, Granny Relda had made a few genuine friends in the community. Among them was a portly sheriff named Ernest Hamstead, who happened to be one of the three not-so-little pigs. He occasionally turned up at the family's door asking for help with unsolved cases, and Granny couldn't resist a mystery.

So here Sabrina sat, leg cramps and all, waiting for burglars to make their move inside the toy shop. There were things she would rather be doing, things she should be doing, like finding her parents. Instead, she and her sister were hiding behind Etch-A-Sketches and cans of Silly String stacked miles high. It was boring work with few distractions. At least she could use the time productively. Sabrina reached into her pocket and pulled out a small flashlight. She flicked its switch to illuminate a book sitting at her feet. She picked it up and started reading—*The Jungle Book* might hold a clue to rescuing her mom and dad. She'd barely read a paragraph before Daphne was grumbling.

"Sabrina," Daphne whispered, "what are you doing? You're going to give us away. Turn off that light."

Sabrina slammed the book closed. There was no arguing with her sister. Daphne had taken to all this silly detective work the way a dog takes to a slice of bologna. Like their grandmother, Daphne loved all of it—the note taking, the stakeouts, the endless research. If only she would use all that energy on something that really mattered—reuniting their family!

A rustling sound drifted across the room, and Sabrina quickly shut off her flashlight. She peered over the stack of dolls and spotted something moving near a display for a hot holiday toy called Don't Tickle the Tiger. Daphne poked her head up, too.

"Do you see anything?" she whispered.

"No. But it's coming from that direction," Sabrina whispered back, pointing toward the rustling. "Wake up Sleepy and see if he smells anything."

Daphne shook Elvis until he staggered to his feet. The big dog's bandages had only recently been removed. He'd had a run-in with a bad guy's boot but had made a full recovery. Still, he was a bit sluggish. He looked around as if he didn't remember where he was.

"You smell any bad guys, Elvis?" Daphne asked softly.

The dog sniffed the air, and his eyes grew wide. He let out a soft whine. The best nose in the Hudson Valley smelled something, indeed.

"Go get 'em, boy!" Daphne cried, and the Great Dane took off like a rocket.

Unfortunately, that was when Sabrina realized Elvis's leash was wrapped around her foot. As the dog howled wildly and tore through the store, he dragged Sabrina, thrashing, behind him,

knocking over stacks of board games and sending balls bouncing in every direction. They emptied puzzle pieces everywhere and sent an army of Slinkys slinking across the floor. Sabrina struggled to grab the leash, but every time she got close to freeing herself, the dog took a wild turn and sent her skidding. She slid into a pile of what felt like sticky leaves. Some clung to her arms and legs, and one glued itself to her forehead.

"Turn on the lights!" Daphne shouted.

When the lights finally came on, Elvis stopped, stood over Sabrina, and barked. The girl sat up and then looked down at herself. She was covered in sticky glue mousetraps, each of which had a tiny little man, no more than a couple of inches high, stuck fast in the glue.

"Hey, let me go!" one of them shouted.

"What's the big idea?" another cried.

"Lilliputians! I knew it!" Granny Relda said, then spotted Sabrina's predicament and laughed. When Sabrina scowled at her, she tried to stop but couldn't.

"Oh, *liebling*," she giggled.

"Who's the sick psychopath who came up with this idea?" one of the Lilliputians shouted indignantly.

Granny leaned down to him and smiled. "Don't worry, with a little vegetable oil we'll have you free in no time."

"But I'm afraid you're under arrest," Sheriff Hamstead said as he stepped out from behind a rack of doll clothes. His puffy pink face beamed proudly as he tugged his trousers up over his massive belly.

The Lilliputians groaned and complained as the sheriff went to work yanking the sticky traps off Sabrina's clothes.

"You have the right to remain silent. Anything you say can and will be used against you in a court of law."

"Ouch!" said Sabrina as the sheriff tugged a glue trap from her forehead.

"I'm not talking, copper," one of the Lilliputians snapped. "And I'm suing you for wrongful arrest."

"Wrongful arrest!" Sheriff Hamstead exclaimed. Unfortunately, when the portly policeman got angry or excited, the magical disguise he used to hide who he really was stopped working. Now his nose vanished and was replaced by a runny pink snout. Two hairy pig ears popped out of the top of his head, and a series of snorts, squeals, and huffs came out of his mouth. Hamstead had nearly completed the change when the security guard from the next store over wandered into the chaos.

"What's going on in here?" the guard asked with a tough, authoritative voice. He was a tall, husky man with a military-style haircut, but when he saw the pig in a police uniform hovering over a dozen tiny men in glue traps, he nearly fainted.

"Oh, dear. We forgot some of the shops have their own security guards," Granny Relda said softly as she reached into her handbag and approached the stunned man.

"Granny, no," Sabrina begged.

"I don't have a choice, Sabrina. It doesn't hurt him," Granny explained, then blew some soft pink dust into the guard's face.

His eyes glazed over as the old woman told him he'd had another ordinary night at work and nothing unusual had occurred. The security guard nodded in agreement.

"Another night at work," he mumbled, falling under the forgetful dust's magic.

Sabrina scowled. She hated when magic was the quick fix to a problem, especially when the problem involved humans.

"The glue traps were a brilliant idea," Sheriff Hamstead said as he drove the family home in his squad car. Granny sat in the front, enjoying his praise, while Sabrina and Daphne were in the back, jockeying with Elvis for seat space. The Lilliputians were locked in the glove compartment, and whenever their complaining got too loud, Hamstead smacked the top of the dashboard with his hand and yelled, "Pipe down!"

"I'm glad we could be of some help," Granny Relda replied. "Geppetto is such a nice old man. It broke my heart to hear he was being robbed, and with Christmas only two weeks away."

"The holidays are difficult for him; he misses his boy," Hamstead said. "It's hard to believe that in two hundred years no one has heard a peep from Pinocchio."

"Wilhelm's journals claim he refused to get on the boat," Granny replied.

"Oh, he got on," Hamstead said. "But as soon as we were out of the marina, he jumped overboard and swam for shore. By the time his father found out, we were too far out to sea to turn back. I suppose if I had been swallowed by a shark, I wouldn't be too eager to go back to sea, either."

"I thought it was a whale," Daphne said.

"No, hon, that was the movie," Granny replied. Sabrina had heard her grandmother explain the difference a hundred times. So much of what the girls thought they knew from seeing all those cartoons was wrong.

"Well, I'm glad to get this case off my plate," the sheriff said. "The mayor's been cutting budgets left and right these days, and I just didn't have the manpower or money to catch the little thieves myself."

"Or to make sure the security guard was off duty so we didn't have to mess with his brain," Sabrina grumbled.

"Sheriff, the Grimms are always at your disposal," Granny Relda said, ignoring Sabrina.

"I appreciate that, Relda, and I wish I could give you the credit for the arrest, but if Mayor Charming found out we've been working together, my backside would be one of those footballs in Geppetto's store," Hamstead said.

"It's our little secret," Granny Relda said with a wink.

"How is Canis?"

Granny's smile faded, and she shifted uncomfortably in her seat. Both Sabrina and Daphne noticed the change and wondered what their grandmother would say about her old friend.

"He's doing just fine."

Sabrina couldn't believe it. In the short time she had known the old woman, Granny Relda had never told a lie. Mr. Canis was not "fine" by a long shot. In fact, he was very, very sick. Three weeks earlier, the girls had learned that Granny's friend, the skinny, grouchy Mr. Canis, was secretly the Big Bad Wolf. When the family battled Jack the Giant Killer over a jar of magic beans, the Wolf bit Jack and tasted the villain's blood. It changed him. When he got home, Canis locked himself inside his bedroom and wouldn't come out. Every night, Sabrina and Daphne heard his painful moans and labored breathing. His horrible cries woke them in the night, and the sounds of him slamming himself against a wall kept their teeth on edge. Mr. Canis was far from "fine."

"That's good to hear," Hamstead said doubtfully.

"I want my phone call!" a little voice cried from the glove compartment. "We were framed!"

The sheriff banged heavily on the dashboard. "Tell it to the judge!"

Sheriff Hamstead pulled his squad car into the driveway of the family's quaint, two-story yellow house. It was very late, and the house was dark. Sabrina opened her door, and Elvis lumbered out, still wearing two Lilliputian-free glue traps on his giant behind. It was bitterly cold, and Sabrina hoped the two adults wouldn't blabber on, as they often did. Granny could talk a person's ear off, but the sheriff just thanked them again and excused himself, claiming he had a mountain of paperwork waiting for him back at the station.

When his taillights were fading down the road, Granny took a giant key ring out of her handbag and went to work unlocking the door. There were more than a dozen locks. Once, Sabrina had believed Granny Relda was just a paranoid shut-in, but in the last three weeks she had seen things that she would never have dreamed possible and now understood why the house was locked so tightly.

When all the locks were turned, the old woman knocked on the door three times and announced to the house that the family was home, making the last magical lock slide back and the door swing open for them.

After cookies, and some vegetable-oil swabbing for Elvis, Granny Relda urged the girls to get to bed. "You've got school tomorrow. I've kept you up too late as it is."

"Actually, Granny," Sabrina replied, feeling her head for a fever that wasn't there, "I think I'm coming down with something. I'd hate to go to school and get everyone sick."

Granny grinned. "Sabrina, it's been three weeks. If you two don't go to school tomorrow, they are going to put me in the jailhouse. Now, up to bed."

Sabrina frowned. School was a waste of time. There were more important things to do.

When Daphne was steadily snoring, Sabrina slowly crawled out of their four-poster bed. The room was once their father's, and his model airplanes still hung from the ceiling. An old catcher's mitt rested on his desk, and his collection of books lined a shelf. Sabrina pulled several of them into her hands, pulled a key ring out from under her mattress, and silently crept into the hallway.

When she reached the door at the end of the hall, she sorted through her keys and found the long brass skeleton key that fit into the lock. Once it was open, she took a quick look around to make sure no one was watching, then slipped inside and closed the door.

The room was completely empty except for a full-length mirror hanging on the far wall and a sliver of moonlight shining through the room's only window. Sabrina stepped up to the mirror and admired her reflection. Her long blond hair and blue eyes glowed a ghostly, milky blue. She tucked some strands behind her ears and rubbed her eyes, then did something most people would think was impossible—she walked directly into the glass and disappeared.

Once she was on the other side, she found herself in an immense room that reminded her of Grand Central Terminal in New York City. Its incredibly long, barrel-vaulted ceiling was supported by towering marble columns, and along each wall were hundreds, maybe even thousands, of doors, each with a golden plaque that revealed what was behind it: TALKING PLANTS, GIANT LIVING CHESS PIECES, BABE THE BLUE OX, MAGICAL ARMOR, and more, all impossibly interesting magical items and creatures collected by the Grimm family for safekeeping. Granny called it the world's biggest walk-in closet. Sabrina called it the Hall of Wonders. She also called it her only hope.

She scanned the hall and spotted a lonely figure sitting in a high-backed chair several yards away.

"Mirror," the girl called to him, "I think I've found something useful."

Mirror, as he was called, was a short, balding man who lived inside the magic mirror. His was the mouth that had proclaimed Snow White "the fairest one of all" to the Wicked Queen. When he spotted Sabrina, he set down the celebrity magazine he was reading and got up from his chair.

"What? No *Hello*? No *How are you? How's the family?*" the little man complained.

"Sorry, Mirror, I don't have a lot of time. I don't want anyone to wake up and find me in here."

"Of course you don't. How would you explain that you've been swiping your grandmother's keys one by one and making copies?"

Sabrina ignored his disapproval.

"I found this thing in Burton's telling of the Arabian Nights," Sabrina said, opening one of her books and handing it to Mirror. He didn't even bother to look at the page.

"Listen, blondie, I assure you, if we had a jinni's lamp, I'd have a lot more hair on my head and we'd all be living in Hawaii. Don't you think that if your grandmother had access to that kind of power, your parents would have already been found?"

Sabrina frowned. It was always the same. She spent days researching ways to rescue her parents from their kidnappers, and every night Mirror shot her ideas down one by one.

"Fine," Sabrina replied, handing Mirror another book she had opened already. "What about this?"

Mirror looked down at the book, flipped it closed to view its cover, and sighed.

"This is not something a kid should be playing with, blondie," he said.

She handed him her set of keys, hoping it had the one she needed.

The little man shrugged and spun around, then headed down

the hallway. "L. Frank Baum was the first to write about the Golden Cap. It's one of the most interesting things the Wicked Witch of the West ever owned and quite an exciting piece for our collection. Most people find her broomstick much more fascinating, but the cap is the most powerful," he continued. "So, you know how it works?"

"Yes, I put it on and recite the magic words, then the monkeys come. They'll do whatever I want them to do."

"Which will be great for you, but I'll be trying to get rid of the monkey smell for months," Mirror said. "That's a special kind of stink."

Mirror stopped at a door labeled MAGICAL HATS, lifted Sabrina's keys, and went to work. A moment later he opened the door and went inside. Sabrina followed and watched him rummage through the room and its thousands of hats and helmets. He made quite a racket moving things around, knocking over top hats and fedoras and bonnets in the process. He let loose an "Aha!" when he found what he wanted.

The Golden Cap was actually yellow, and it held a can of soda on each side with tubes that ran down to the mouth. On the front of the hat the words EMERALD CITY GREEN SOX were printed in big green letters. Mirror dusted it off and handed it to Sabrina.

"This is the Golden Cap? The one the Wicked Witch of the West used to summon flying monkeys?" she asked in disbelief.

"The witch was a huge sports fan," Mirror replied. "She won her fantasy football league four years in a row."

"You've got to be kidding me," Sabrina said.

"Afraid not. The magic instructions are inside."

The girl read a slip taped inside and scowled. In the short time since she had discovered that fairy tales were real, the one thing she saw over and over again was that everything from Oz was completely wacko. She put the cap on her head, and, following the ridiculous instructions, she lifted her right leg and began the crazy spell.

"Ep-pe, pep-pe, kak-ke."

Mirror turned away and snickered.

"Don't laugh," Sabrina said, lowering her leg and lifting the other. "Hil-lo, hol-lo, hel-lo."

"I wish I had a camera." The little man giggled.

"Ziz-zy, zuz-zy, zik!" the girl said, now standing on both feet. Suddenly, her ears filled with the sound of a hundred flapping wings. Monkeys materialized out of thin air, hovering overhead and held aloft by leathery black wings. Sabrina now understood why Mirror had warned her about the monkey smell. They were a ripe bunch. She would have pinched her nose if she hadn't been afraid it was rude.

One of the monkeys, wearing a beanie with a bright blue ball on top, took her hand and gave it a sloppy kiss.

"What is your bidding, master?" it asked in a deep, other-worldly voice.

"OK, uh, Mr. Monkey . . . uh, I need you to go fetch my parents," she said. Sabrina was still not used to talking animals.

The monkeys screamed with glee and clapped their hands as if she were promising them bananas. They circled the room, slamming into one another, but ultimately they landed at her feet. Their leader's face was full of confusion.

"What's wrong?" Sabrina asked.

"Your wish cannot be granted. Great magic blocks our path," he said, and as quickly as the monkeys had appeared, they were gone.

"Why not?" Sabrina shouted angrily. She took the obnoxious magic hat off her head and shook it, but the monkeys did not return. She was so tired of being disappointed. How many more dead ends could she come up against? It wasn't fair. She handed the Golden Cap back to Mirror, and the little man gave her a sad, pitying smile. He placed it back on its shelf, then locked the door behind him before giving her back her keys.

"We'll keep trying," he promised.

She sighed and walked silently back through the portal. Once she found herself on the other side, she turned and eyed her sad reflection.

"Mirror?" she called out softly. A blue mist filled the glass, and the little man's other face appeared. It was thick, muscular, and foreboding.

"You know how it works," he said.

"Mirror, mirror, near and far, show me where my parents are," the girl said.

The face disappeared, and Sabrina's slumbering parents took its place. Henry and Veronica Grimm were lying on a bed in the dark, fast asleep, which was exactly how she had found them the day before, and the day before that. They never moved, never even turned in bed. It was almost like they were porcelain statues. They looked vulnerable lying there surrounded by darkness.

"I won't let another Christmas go by without you. I'll find a way to bring you home," Sabrina promised as she reached out as if to touch them. Her hand dipped into the magic mirror's reflective surface, and her parents' image rippled the way a pond does when a stone is thrown into it. Sabrina stared at them until they faded away.

"Same time tomorrow night?" Mirror asked as his face reappeared.

"See you then," Sabrina said, wiping the tears from her cheeks. She tiptoed back down the hallway, but just as she reached her bedroom, she heard a painful groan coming from Mr. Canis's room. He was having another difficult night. She stood in the hallway listening to his breathing, less concerned about his suffering than she was worried that at any moment the door would explode and the Big Bad Wolf would snatch her in his claws. What would they do if Mr. Canis lost control of the monster inside of him? What if the old man wasn't strong enough to keep the wolf locked away?

"Go to bed, child," a voice growled. "Or are you going to huff and puff and blow the door down?" The voice startled Sabrina—it sounded like a combination of Canis and the Wolf—and she quickly darted into her bedroom and closed the door tight.

2

THERE WERE THREE THINGS THAT SABRINA TOOK great pride in: One, she had successfully arm-wrestled and beaten every boy at the orphanage (including two extremely humiliated janitors); two, she wasn't afraid of heights; and three, she wasn't a sissy. But when one wakes up to find a giant hairy spider crawling on one's face, one should be allowed to throw a hissy fit. So Sabrina did just that.

Her bloodcurdling screams woke Daphne, who saw the spider and screamed, too, which made the whole thing that much more horrible for Sabrina—so she screamed even louder, which caused her sister to scream at her sister's scream, resulting in a mini-concert of hysteria that went on and on for nearly five minutes.

Granny Relda burst into their bedroom with Elvis at her side. Her face was covered in a mossy-green mud mask that she swore kept her looking young. But her mud mask wasn't nearly as star-tling as the deadly, sharp broadsword she held in her hand and the fierce battle cry she bellowed. Her sudden appearance renewed the screaming.

Scanning the room for attackers, the old woman said, "My goodness, *lieblings*—what is the matter?"

"That!" Sabrina and Daphne shouted in unison, pointing at a black tarantula the size of a baked potato. Its eight long, hairy legs and vicious-looking pincers clicked and snapped as it leaped off the bed and clung to a nearby curtain.

"Oh, children, it's just a spider," Granny Relda said as she crossed the room and picked the creepy-crawly thing up with her bare hands. Daphne squealed and crawled under her blanket to hide.

"Just a spider?" Sabrina cried. "You could put a saddle on that thing!"

"He's South American, I believe," Granny said, petting the spider like it was a kitten. "You're a long way from home, friend. How did you find your way here?"

"Like you have to ask!" Sabrina cried.

"Now, now," the old woman said, "he's harmless."

"Is it gone yet?" Daphne's muffled voice came from under the covers. "Has it been squished?"

"He's going to pay, Granny!" Sabrina promised.

"Girls, Puck's just being a boy. Brothers do these kinds of things to their sisters all the time."

"He's not our brother!" Sabrina shouted as she crawled out of bed and stomped across the room toward the door. If Granny wasn't going to do anything about Puck's endless pranks, she'd take care of it herself.

"Where are you going?" Granny Relda asked.

"To introduce Puck's face to my fist," the girl said, marching past the old woman and out the door.

"Don't leave me in here with the spider!" Daphne begged.

Puck, like Mr. Canis, was an Everafter, but weird on a whole different level. He was a four-thousand-year-old fairy in the body of an eleven-year-old boy. Rude, selfish, smelly, and obnoxious, he taunted Sabrina mercilessly: dumping a bucket of paint on her, rubbing her toothbrush in red-pepper flakes, filling her pockets with bloodworms, and putting something in her shoes that still made her shudder when she recalled its smell. Puck also had a slew of magical pranks. He could shape-shift into any animal and several inanimate objects. Sabrina couldn't count how many times she had gone to sit in a chair and tumbled over when it pulled itself out from under her. Why Granny Relda adored Puck was beyond comprehension, especially with his well-documented history. Everyone from William Shakespeare to Rudyard Kipling had written about Puck's exploits, yet Granny treated him as if he were one of the family. She had even invited him to live with them. Now Sabrina was determined to make the Trickster King wish he had declined the invitation.

She marched down the hall to his bedroom and pounded on the door.

"C'mon out, Puck!" she shouted.

There was no response, so she knocked again, adding a swift kick to accentuate the point. Still, he did not respond. She eyed the OFF LIMITS sign the boy had nailed to the door. Everyone deserved their privacy, but if he wasn't coming out, she'd have to go in, whether he liked it or not.

Sabrina opened the door and stepped inside . . . and was struck speechless. Puck's room was impossible. There were trees and grass and a stone path and a waterfall that spilled into a lagoon. There was an actual sky with clouds and kites where the ceiling should have been. In the center of a clearing was a wrestling ring in which a kangaroo wearing boxing gloves and shorts sat lazily waiting for his next challenger. A roller coaster sailed on a track above Sabrina, and an ice-cream truck was parked to one side. In the center of it all was Puck, perched on an enormous throne, wearing his stupid golden crown. He was eating an ice-cream cone that held half a dozen different-flavored scoops, all of which were dripping down his arm. The Three Little Pigs had used nails, hammers, and magic to build Puck's bedroom. Sabrina had no idea it would be so amazing.

She was so astonished by her surroundings that she failed to notice the metal plate beneath her feet. Her weight triggered the release of an egg, which rolled down a narrow track and fell onto a rusty nail, cracking its shell in half. The drippings emptied into a skillet, which tilted and struck a match, igniting a gas burner on a stove. The egg crackled and popped in the heat, causing steam to rise, which, in turn, filled a balloon that rose into the air. The balloon was connected to a string that pulled a small lever, which tipped a bucket of water into a drinking glass sitting on the high end of a seesaw. The seesaw tilted downward from the weight, untying a rope that held a heavy sandbag. The sandbag fell onto a bright red button, and then it all came to a stop.

"What is that supposed to do?" Sabrina asked.

A buzzer drowned out her voice, and before Sabrina knew it, she was catapulted off the metal plate and up, up, up, through the air and then down, down, down, into a large wooden vat of goo. There was an enormous splash.

"Doesn't anyone knock around here?" Puck complained when Sabrina finally fought her way to the surface.

"What is this stuff?" she cried as she struggled through the vat of thick white mush filled with several floating dark chunks. The stink of it nearly made Sabrina barf.

"It's a big tub of glue and buttermilk, of course," the boy said, as if it were obvious. "With some bread-and-butter pickles added for flavor. It's quite stinky. I use it punish invaders. You did read the OFF LIMITS sign, correct?"

"You're going to pay for this, Puck!" Sabrina screamed as she

struggled out of the tub. Once she was on her feet, she wiped her face as well as she could and flared her nostrils.

"There she is . . . Miss America," the prankster sang. He tossed his huge ice-cream cone into the wrestling ring, and the kangaroo lapped it up happily. Then the boy sprang into the air, and two massive pink-streaked insect wings popped out of his back. He soared over Sabrina, giggling at her misfortune.

"Come down here, you smelly little freak!" Sabrina shouted.

"Grimm, you seem angry," Puck said.

Sabrina put up her fist. "Let me show you how angry I am."

"You want to fight me? Human, I'm royalty. A prince fights like a prince."

He flew back to his throne and swooped down, snatching two wooden swords from a collection he kept in a pile nearby. He tossed one at Sabrina's feet, then floated effortlessly to the ground.

Sabrina grabbed her weapon and held its handle tightly. If she could get a good whack at Puck with it, he'd hurt for days.

"En garde!" Puck said, waving his weapon in front of him.

The two children circled each other. Sabrina wasted no time thrusting her sword at the boy, who spun easily, dodging her attack. While she was off balance, Puck flew toward her, trying to strike her arm. But Sabrina shifted her weight and hit him on the top of his head.

"Dirty little snotface!" the boy cried as he rubbed his sore noggin. "Someone's been learning."

"Charge at me again, and you'll see what else I've learned, horsebreath!" Sabrina threatened.

Puck charged at her, swinging his wooden sword, only to have her block his attack. She took a swipe at his belly, missing him by less than an inch.

"Tsk, tsk. Looks like you haven't learned the most important lesson of all." He laughed. "Always protect your butt." He smacked Sabrina on the backside with the flat of his weapon. The blow felt like a dozen honeybee stings.

"You're as slow as you are ugly," the boy taunted.

"You miserable little stink-pig!" Sabrina screamed, wildly slashing at him.

He dodged each sloppy attack, leaping and flying out of the way, even flipping completely over her head. When he landed, he jammed his sword into her back and chuckled. "Temper, temper," he said. "You've really got to get ahold of your anger. It beats you every time."

Sabrina tossed her sword down angrily and spun around on him with fists clenched. Seeing her fury, Puck did what anybody would do when facing an angry Sabrina Grimm—he ran. She chased him around the lagoon while he laughed. He led her into some heavy brush, teasing her with every step, until they came out the other side and ran right into Granny Relda. The old woman stood over them, and her expression, or what they could see of it behind her mud mask, was disapproving.

"Old lady!" he cried. "Your face! You've been kissing hobgoblins!"

"I've had enough of this nonsense," Granny said as the dirty boy scampered to his feet and hid behind her. "The two of you need to learn to get along."

"She's the one who's trespassing. She came in here to kill me. Is this about the chain saw? It was only supposed to scare her," he said. "If someone got hurt, it wasn't my fault."

"Chain saw?" Sabrina cried.

"Puck, we're talking about the spider," Granny Relda said.

"Oh, the spider. How did it go off? Did it scare them out of their wits?" he asked. "Which one of them wet the bed?"

"I know you didn't mean any harm," the old woman said. "But the girls do have school today, and it would have been nice to have had a quiet, chaos-free morning for once."

Puck looked into her face as if she were speaking another language. "And what would be the fun in that?"

"Let's back up!" Sabrina demanded. "What chain saw?"

Granny took the boy's hand and placed the furry tarantula in it. "Let's put this somewhere safe."

Puck took the spider and rubbed its furry back softly. "It's OK, little guy. Did the big, ugly girl scare you? I know she's gruesome, but you're safe now."

Sabrina growled.

"Will someone please give me an update on the spider?" Daphne shouted from the doorway. The little girl rubbed the sleep out of her eyes, then looked around with amazement. "Holy cow! You've got an ice-cream truck in here!"

"Daphne, don't stand there!" her sister warned, but the egg was already cooking and the balloon was already rising.

"Sabrina, why do you look like a walking booger?" the little girl asked as the seesaw fell. The alarm sounded, and the catapult fired Daphne into the air. She sailed into the vat of goo, then struggled to stand up as slime dripped down her face.

"What is this?" she asked.

"Glue and buttermilk!" Puck shouted.

"And bread-and-butter pickles," Sabrina added, picking a squishy slice off her forehead.

Daphne's face curled up in confusion as if she couldn't get her brain around the idea. Then she grinned.

"I want to do it again!" She laughed.

Granny Relda helped Daphne out of the sticky soup.

"Look at the two of you," Granny said. "You're a mess."

"We can't go to school today!" Sabrina said. Suddenly, her anger at Puck faded. "I can do more research!"

"Oh, *lieblings*, you've already missed so much. I don't want you to get behind," Granny said.

"We'll just go tomorrow, then," Sabrina suggested.

Before Granny Relda could respond, Mr. Canis appeared at the door, fully dressed in his oversized suit. He looked exhausted and feverish, even frailer than usual.

"The children have a visitor," he said, leaning unsteadily against the doorframe.

"Thank you, Mr. Canis," Granny Relda said, sounding quite motherly. "I'm sorry if it disturbed you."

"You may not want to make her wait," he said.

"Her?" Granny Relda asked. Then her face fell. "Oh, her. Thank you, old friend. I can handle it."

The old man nodded and shuffled back toward his room.

"Who's here to see them?" Puck asked enviously.

Sabrina shrugged and turned to ask her grandmother, but the old woman was already hurrying out the door.

The children followed her eagerly, down the stairs and into the living room, where they saw a skinny old woman in a drab business suit snooping through their bookshelves. She picked up a volume with her bony hand and scrutinized the title. Sabrina knew the book. It was called *Mermaids Are People, Too*. The skinny woman tossed it aside and turned to face them, but Sabrina knew her face before she saw it. It was the worst face she had ever seen.

"Good morning, girls," Ms. Smirt said. "Did you miss me?"

3

INERVA SMIRT HADN'T CHANGED SINCE THE last time the girls had seen her. The caseworker was still gaunt and tired-looking. Her bones still poked out of her clothes as if they were trying to escape her body, and she wore the same angry scowl on her face. She stared scornfully down her long, hooked nose at the girls. When her eyes swept over Puck, he shuddered as if he were caught in a winter chill.

"My, my, my," she said.

"Ms. Smirt, what a pleasant surprise," Granny Relda said without much conviction. "It's so nice to see you again."

"I doubt that, Mrs. Grimm. Girls, get your things," Ms. Smirt said. "You're going back to the orphanage."

Daphne slipped her hand into her sister's and squeezed so hard, it hurt.

"What in heavens for?" Granny Relda demanded.

Ms. Smirt waved a hand toward the girls, who were still dripping with glue and buttermilk. "It's not obvious? Mrs. Grimm, you've been completely negligent."

"What does *negligent* mean?" Daphne asked.

"It means she's doing a terrible job looking after you," Ms. Smirt snapped, interrupting Sabrina, who usually answered Daphne's vocabulary questions. "It means she's fallen far short of what the state requires of her. It means she is unfit!"

"That's not true!" Daphne cried.

"You two haven't had a day of school since you arrived," the caseworker continued. "I sent your grandmother a letter reminding her about the law, but I never heard back. I sent another, and then another, and then another. But still I heard nothing. So, because she can't find the time to put pen to paper and assure me that you two will be educated, I had to get on a five a.m. off-peak train and sit next to a man who sniffed his own armpits for two hours. Imagine how it feels to find that my suspicions are true and that not only have you two not been in school for almost a month, you obviously haven't been in a bathtub, either!"

"Who is this woman?" Puck asked. "Is she a witch?"

"Her name's Minerva Smirt. She is our caseworker from the orphanage," Sabrina answered.

"Cranky old buzzard, isn't she?" the boy replied. "She has to be a witch."

Smirt growled and flared her nostrils.

Sabrina smiled. *Puck sure has his moments*, she thought.

"And who are you supposed to be?" Ms. Smirt asked. "The king of snot-nosed delinquents?"

Puck smiled. "Finally, someone around here has heard of me!"

"This is my nephew visiting from . . . uh . . . Akron, Ohio," Granny said as she snatched Puck's crown off his head. "Ms. Smirt, I assure you the girls are going to go to school today. We've gotten a little sidetracked with visiting and such."

Suddenly, Sabrina felt regret for all the excuses she had given her grandmother to delay school: stomach viruses, headaches, sore teeth, deep depressions, phantom pains. The truth was, she and her sister had agreed, school could wait, at least until their mother and father were home safe.

"You understand, Ms. Smirt," Granny Relda continued.

"I understand completely. You are incompetent!" The caseworker grabbed the sisters roughly by the arms and pulled them toward the door. "Girls, grab your coats. We've got a train to catch. We'll send for the rest of your things."

Just then, Elvis trotted into the room. He spotted Ms. Smirt, and his usually happy face instantly turned ferocious. He charged the caseworker, sending her tumbling backward over a pile of books, then stood over her, baring his teeth and growling.

"Get this thing away from me, or we'll make a stop at the

pound, too!" Ms. Smirt shouted, waving a book at the dog in a fruitless attempt to intimidate him. Granny Relda stepped forward to help the woman, but Sabrina and Daphne stopped her. Instead, the girls stood on either side of the dog and looked down at their caseworker.

"Call him off!"

"Not until we come to an understanding," Sabrina said. "My sister and I are going to go upstairs and get cleaned up. We're going to get dressed, and our grandmother is going to take us to school. You are going enroll us in school, then go back to New York City, alone."

"You don't get to make the rules, young lady," Ms. Smirt snapped.

"You're absolutely right. We don't get to make the rules. Elvis does. So, Elvis, what do you think we should do?" Sabrina asked.

Elvis barked viciously.

"I think Elvis likes this plan," Daphne said, patting the big dog on his head. "If you disagree, I suppose you can try to change his mind."

Elvis grunted aggressively.

Ms. Smirt stared at the girls for a long moment, then furrowed her brow. "Fine! But get this thing off me. It's slobbering on my suit," she snarled.

♡

Sabrina knew that school was just going to be another distraction from finding her parents, but she tried to put a positive spin on it. Sixth grade offered her something that Granny Relda's house didn't—normal people. She could use some normal in her life. If Ferryport Landing Elementary was like other schools, it would be full of dull teachers and glassy-eyed kids, all watching the clock tick slowly until it was time to go home. There would be no Big Bad Wolf, flying boys, or talking pigs.

As Sabrina and her family, accompanied by Ms. Smirt, stepped up the path to the front door, she anticipated her first day of mind-numbing dullness. She would melt into the crowd and do her best not to draw any attention to herself. She wouldn't join any clubs or raise her hand but would drift through the day like an invisible girl. She would find some kids to befriend, and they would sit together at lunchtime and maybe pass notes in class. Just like normal kids. It was going to be one long, humdrum, happy experience.

Unfortunately, Smirt was ruining Sabrina's plan. It's hard to be just another face in the crowd when you're being dragged down the hallway by your ear. Not that it was entirely Ms. Smirt's fault that Sabrina was catching so many curious eyes. Even after three vigorous washings, her hair was still full of the goo from Puck's booby trap. Her locks stuck out in a thousand different directions like an excited octopus. Daphne, on the other hand, had sculpted her hair into an old-fashioned beehive style that spiraled high on her head, straight out of the 1950s. Inside the sticky tower, the little girl had inserted pencils and pens, a ruler, a protractor, two gummy erasers, and a package of peanut-butter crackers for later. Only Daphne herself knew what else might be hiding inside. By the time they got to the main office, Sabrina was sure every kid in the school thought that Ferryport Landing Elementary was now enrolling escaped mental patients.

"Excuse me! I'm Minerva Smirt from the New York City Department of Child Welfare," Ms. Smirt said, pounding impatiently on a bell that sat on the counter. Two middle-aged secretaries were busy spraying bug spray into a corner of the room. The one wearing thick glasses smacked at something with a magazine, while the chubby one stomped on it like an Irish folk dancer.

"I think it's dead," the chubby one said as she bent over to get a better look.

Smirt rang the bell again. "I'm in a hurry," the caseworker said. "I need to enroll these two orphans."

"We are not orphans!" Sabrina and Daphne said in unison.

Ms. Smirt pinched them each on the shoulder for arguing.

The bespectacled secretary crossed the room, snatched the bell away, and stuffed it into a drawer. "How can I help you?" she asked, forcing a smile onto her face.

"Are you deaf? I said I need to enroll these two girls," Smirt snapped.

"I'll see if our guidance counselor, Mr. Sheepshank, is available," the secretary replied as she eyed the children in bewilderment. Shaking her head, she stepped over to a door and knocked on it lightly.

"Sir, we have some new students . . . I think," she said, turning back and eyeing the girls.

"How delightful! Please send them in right away," a happy voice called from within the room.

The secretary waved the group into the office and closed the door.

Mr. Sheepshank was a little man dressed in a green suit and a bow tie with smiley faces on it. He had a round, full, friendly face with freckled cheeks and ginger hair. When he smiled, little wrinkle lines formed in the corners of his glittering eyes. Sabrina thought he looked a bit like a cartoon.

"Good morning, ladies. I'm Casper Sheepshank, your school counselor," the man said cheerily. "Welcome to Ferryport Landing Elementary."

"It's nice to meet—" Granny started, before Smirt cut her off.

"I'm Minerva . . . Minerva Smirt from the New York City Department of Child Welfare," she said, then did something Sabrina had never seen her do before: She smiled.

"It's a pleasure to meet you," the guidance counselor replied, taking her hand and shaking it vigorously. "And who are these lovely ladies?"

"Introduce yourselves, girls," Ms. Smirt said, giggling.

"I'm Sabrina Grimm," Sabrina said.

Sheepshank seized her hand and gave her the same joint-jarring treatment he had given to Ms. Smirt.

"I'm Daphne Grimm," Daphne chirped.

"Grimm? You wouldn't happen to be related to Henry Grimm?" the counselor asked.

"He's my son," Granny Relda said. "And these are his daughters."

"He went to school here with us, too," Mr. Sheepshank said. "I remember him quite clearly. A bit of a mischief maker but very charming. I expect it runs in the family?"

Unsure of how to respond, the girls said nothing. After a long, uncomfortable pause Sheepshank chuckled and winked at Sabrina.

"The girls were in my custody for a year and a half until we placed them here in Ferryport Landing with Relda," Ms. Smirt explained. "Unfortunately, Mrs. Grimm has not taken their education seriously, and they've been out of school for a month."

Granny Relda blushed.

"Better late than never," the counselor said with a laugh. "Please, have a seat." He pulled some paperwork out of a desk drawer and began to write.

"Casper," Ms. Smirt said, unbuttoning her top blouse button as if she were suddenly warm. "I wouldn't be able to sleep at night if I didn't warn you about these two. They are quite a handful. I tried to place them in good homes more than a dozen times, and each time it ended in chaos and grief. Nothing was ever good enough for them. They ran away from one foster home just because they were asked to help around the house."

"It wasn't a house! It was a stable," Sabrina said defensively.

"A pony got into my suitcase and ate all my underpants," Daphne added.

"They're also very argumentative," Ms. Smirt said, reaching down and giving each girl a hard pinch on the leg.

"Mr. Sheepshank, I've had the girls for three weeks. I think Ms. Smirt's assessment is a little biased. I have found the girls to be delightful and curious."

Mr. Sheepshank smiled warmly at the girls. "Here at Ferryport Landing Elementary we like to set our sights on the future. Our motto is, *Everyone deserves a second chance.*"

"Well, I'll tell you, Casper, as a professional who's worked with children for almost thirty years, I'd say a second chance is the last thing a child needs. What most of them need is a swift kick in the—"

"Thanks for the warning, Ms. Smirt," the counselor interrupted.

"Please, call me Minerva," the skinny woman purred. "You'll need their transcripts, of course. I could bring them up Friday. It's just a two-hour trip. Maybe we could discuss their files over dinner."

There was a long, uncomfortable silence. Mr. Sheepshank blushed and shuffled some papers on his desk.

"That's not necessary. Just drop them in the mail when you get a chance," he said at last. "Well, I'd better get these girls started. I trust you can find your way out, Ms. Smirt?"

The caseworker shifted in her chair, and her face turned red with frustration. "Of course," she said. She reached into her handbag and took out a card. "Here's my office number if you need any help with them. My cell phone is on there, too."

Sabrina gazed down at the caseworker's handbag. When she spotted a book entitled *Finding Mr. Right*, the unsettling truth about what she was witnessing revealed itself. Ms. Smirt was flirting. An image of the two grown-ups kissing flashed in Sabrina's mind, and she blanched as if she had just witnessed a car crash.

"Well, Susie . . . Debbie . . . I'm off," the skinny woman said as she got up from her chair.

"Sabrina," Sabrina said. Her sympathy vanished.

"Daphne," Daphne added.

Ms. Smirt gave Granny Relda a sour look. "Mrs. Grimm."

"Ms. Smirt," the old woman said.

Smirt turned at the door. "Maybe we'll talk again, Casper . . ."

Mr. Sheepshank smiled but said nothing. He only stared at her as if he were a deer caught in front of a speeding truck. After several way-too-long, awkward moments of silence, Ms. Smirt stepped into the hallway.

"That was so gross," Daphne whispered.

Granny reached into her handbag and took out a sheet of paper, then placed it before the counselor.

"Mr. Sheepshank, here are a list of emergency numbers in case there is a problem. I've also taken the liberty of including the number for the local police and fire stations, as well as nine-one-one, and poison control—"

"Mrs. Grimm, are you feeling a little separation anxiety?"

"What's separation anxiety mean?" Daphne asked.

"It means she's having a little freak-out over leaving us here," Sabrina asked.

Granny nodded. "I suppose I am. I just got the girls into my life, and, well, a grandmother worries."

"Please, rest assured that they are in excellent care," Mr. Sheepshank replied, tapping Granny's sheet of phone numbers. "But if there is an international incident before lunch, I promise to call the state department right away. Now, I suppose we should get you two to class."

Granny shed a few tears as she hugged the girls good-bye.

"It's just school," Daphne said.

"I know. I'm being silly. I just love having you around," the old woman said before she headed for the exit.

The girls and the counselor followed her to the door and waved good-bye.

Mr. Sheepshank led them down a hallway. "Ladies, I think you're going to love it here at Ferryport Landing Elementary. The first day of school can be a difficult adjustment. But I want you to know that if there are any bumps in the road—for example, someone you can't get along with or a teacher who's given you too much homework—I'm the man to come to. Feel free to stop by my office anytime you want. My job is to listen, and my door is always open."

Sabrina was surprised by his attitude. In the dozen or so schools she had been in over the last few years, no one had ever spoken to her like this. She was used to lectures about being responsible and the value of hard work, but Mr. Sheepshank seemed to understand how hard it was to be a kid.

Just then a tall, dark-haired man in a gray suit rushed down the hall toward them. He had a long, lean, ruddy face that made his crooked nose look enormous. Because he was upset, his big, bushy eyebrows bounced around on his forehead like excited caterpillars. "Mr. Sheepshank!" he shouted in a German accent not unlike Granny Relda's. "We are due for a conversation!"

"Children, this is your principal, Mr. Hamelin," the guidance counselor said, ignoring the man's frustration. "Mr. Hamelin, I'd like to introduce you to our new students, Sabrina and Daphne Grimm."

"My grandmother says hello," Sabrina said.

Principal Hamelin stopped in his tracks and cocked a curious eyebrow, suddenly aware of who the girls were and how they knew him. Granny Relda had told them both that there were a couple of Everafters working at Ferryport Landing Elementary: Snow White, who was a teacher, and the principal, Mr. Hamelin, who was also known as the Pied Piper of Hamelin. Granny had even told them the story of the Pied Piper, how by using his magical bagpipes he'd enchanted a horde of rats to drown themselves.

"Of course, of course," Hamelin said, forcing a smile onto his face. "I was told you'd be coming. Welcome to Ferryport Landing Elementary. Um, Mr. Sheepshank, I need to discuss the . . . uh . . . textbook shortage."

"My pleasure, Mr. Hamelin. Just let me get the Grimms settled into their classes," the counselor replied, leading the girls down the hallway. Soon, they stopped in front of a classroom, and Mr. Sheepshank patted Daphne on the shoulder. "This is your class."

The girls peered through the window in the door and saw a stunningly beautiful woman with hair the color of midnight and eyes as big as the sea. Her teeth were so dazzlingly white, Sabrina had to shield her eyes from the glare.

"Daphne, your teacher's name is Ms. White," Sheepshank said.

Daphne put the palm of her hand into her mouth and bit on it. It was an odd little habit she had when she was very excited or happy.

"This is so great, I might barf," the little girl said giddily. She had prayed on hands and knees each night that she would be in the legendary beauty's class. It looked as if someone had been listening.

"Don't put any crayons in your nose," Sabrina joked as Mr. Sheepshank led her sister into the room. Daphne stuck her tongue out in reply.

As the guidance counselor introduced Daphne to her new teacher and class, Sabrina studied Ms. White through the open door. She and Mr. Hamelin were both Everafters, and both seemed very nice. Granny had high opinions of them . . . but could they be trusted? It suddenly dawned on Sabrina that either one of them could have been involved in her parents' disappearance. A wave of suspicion rolled over her, and anger bubbled up from her belly. Maybe Ms. White and Mr. Hamelin were working together. Maybe they were in the Scarlet Hand. She needed to know. She was going to march right into the room and confront Ms. White. She was going to demand she confess!

"Sabrina, are you feeling OK?" Mr. Sheepshank asked when he joined her in the hall. She looked up into his face and shook off her rage. She was stunned at her anger and the thoughts that came with it. It was like she had fallen under some dark spell, and now that it was gone, she had a pounding headache. "Yes, I'm OK."

"You look a little pale. Check with the school nurse if you feel ill," the counselor instructed, then directed her down the hall and up a flight of stairs. On the second floor was another long hallway full of classrooms. They stopped at the first door, and Sheepshank opened it. He turned to Sabrina and gave her a warm smile. "I think this might just be the perfect homeroom for you."

"Mr. Grumpner," he said as he stepped into the classroom. "I'd like to introduce you and the class to a new student. Her name is Sabrina Grimm. She and her sister just moved to Ferryport Landing from New York City."

"She looks like she stuck a fork into a light socket," a boy called from the middle of the room. He was short, with wiry black hair and big bug eyes. A few kids snickered, but most of the class seemed to be asleep or about to doze off.

"Toby, shut up," Grumpner growled.

The boy's face turned red, and he looked as if he might actually get out of his seat and charge at his teacher, but he sat still, grumbling under his breath. A pretty girl with platinum blond hair and big green eyes put her hand on the boy's arm, and it seemed to calm him down.

Grumpner turned his attention back to Sabrina. He was an old man with saggy jowls and thin, charcoal-colored hair. He looked like a deflating birthday-party balloon found in the garage a week after the fun is over.

"Sit," he said gruffly as he pointed to several empty desks in the last row. Then he turned back to the guidance counselor. "Sheepshank, what is wrong with these kids? Half of them are asleep, and the other half are between naps!"

"I'm sure you'll find a way to get them motivated, Mr. Grumpner," the counselor said as he waved to Sabrina and left the room. "After all, you're one of our finest teachers."

The compliment did little to calm the old man down. He huffed and turned back to the class.

"Good luck, Sabrina," Mr. Sheepshank said, then turned and left.

"Open your books to page one-forty-two," Grumpner growled as he tossed a ratty textbook at Sabrina. She caught it and hurried to an empty desk, then scrambled to find the page, only to find that it and dozens more were ripped out of the book.

"You need to read this page carefully, morons," Grumpner threatened. "Tomorrow you're going to have a quiz on it."

Sabrina slowly raised her hand.

"What is it, Grimm?"

"That page is missing," she mumbled.

Grumpner's face turned red. Even from the back of the room, Sabrina could spot a throbbing vein in his forehead preparing to explode. Before he could blow up and kill them all, a short, pudgy boy ran into the classroom. He rushed past the teacher and hurried down Sabrina's aisle, where he slipped behind a desk and opened a book.

"Wendell!" Grumpner bellowed at the top of his lungs. The chubby boy looked up from his desk, wiped his nose with a handkerchief, and looked genuinely surprised by the teacher's anger. It took all of Sabrina's willpower not to break out laughing at the boy's dumbfounded expression.

"Yes, Mr. Grumpner," Wendell replied.

"You are late, again," the teacher said.

"I'm sorry. I forgot to set my alarm clock," the boy said meekly.

"You forgot?" Grumpner exploded. "Well, that's just great! I bet you didn't forget breakfast this morning! Everyone can see that! Maybe we should cover your alarm clock with candy and French fries; then you'd never forget to set it!"

"I don't see how weight-shaming me is connected to tardiness," Wendell said.

The old man stomped down the aisle and roughly pulled the boy out of his seat. He dragged him to the front of the room so everyone could see his humiliation.

"Do you know why you are always late, Wendell?" Mr.

Grumpner asked. "It's because you are a worthless, slow-minded moron. Isn't that right?"

This woke up the class, which roared with laughter. Toby, the bug-eyed boy, nearly fell out of his chair giggling.

Before Wendell could answer, Grumpner shoved a piece of chalk into his hand and spun him toward the chalkboard.

"And you are going to write it until the end of this class. You might think that you get a free pass around here because you're the principal's son, but I'm not afraid of your father. I have tenure. Get started!"

As Wendell turned to the chalkboard, Sabrina felt the air rush out of her lungs. Was it true? Was Wendell Mr. Hamelin's son? If it was, he was the child of an Everafter! Sabrina knew that many in the secret community were building new lives in America, but she never imagined they would start families. She looked around the class, eyeing each student carefully. Were there any more Everafter kids in her class?

As Sabrina drifted from class to class, she had only one thought on her mind: She had to tell Daphne what she had learned about Wendell. Unfortunately, she didn't see her sister in the halls. What she did see troubled her, though. Everyone was angry. Mr. Grumpner wasn't the only teacher on the verge of a nervous breakdown. In fact, the entire staff was a collection of bullying, screaming nightmares who enjoyed tormenting their students and coworkers. They shouted through most of their classes, dishing out detentions like scoops of ice cream.

The children, however, were walking zombies. They slept through the lectures, and none of their homework was done. In most of Sabrina's classes, at least half the students were too drowsy to notice when the teacher was talking to them. Even in PE, the kids staggered around exhausted, which was very unfortunate, because it was one place they really needed to be alert. Their teacher, Ms. Spangler, also known as Spangler the Strangler, was a bulky cow of a woman with a ponytail and an evil glint in her eye. She apparently only knew how to teach one game—dodgeball. Sabrina considered herself to be pretty good at the game; she had been the last kid standing many times at her school in NYC. So in Ms. Spangler's class, when the first rubber ball smacked her in the head so hard, her brains rattled, she knew something about this dodgeball game was different. Her name was Natalie.

Natalie was a knuckle-dragging hulk with ratty brown hair. She was insanely strong and seemed to get a sick thrill out of pelting kids with her lightning-fast pitch. Toby, the bug-eyed boy from her homeroom, kept close to Natalie, and together they were vicious. They whipped balls relentlessly, and when a kid fell down, the duo pummeled him or her mercilessly. Ms. Spangler encouraged the mercilessness. She ran around the gymnasium blowing her whistle and pointing out the weaknesses of the other players to Natalie and Toby, urging them to target the pudgy, the small, the slow, and the awkward. Whenever a kid was hit and eliminated, Ms. Spangler clapped as happily as a child on Christmas morning.

There was only one other kid in the class who had the energy to defend herself. Sabrina recognized her from Mr. Grumpner's class, too. The pretty blonde who was able to calm Toby's temper got no preferential treatment from him in PE. He and Natalie targeted her with just as much zeal as they had the others, but the girl managed to duck out of the way, dodging and jumping with incredible skill. Eventually, though, even she grew tired, and she was eliminated by a shot to the back. She joined the battered and abused kids waiting on the sidelines. When she spotted Sabrina, she smiled and waved. It was the first act of kindness Sabrina experienced the whole day.

By lunchtime, Sabrina had recovered from her beating, and she went looking for her sister. She needed to tell Daphne what she had learned about Wendell and to see if her sister was aware of any other Everafter children who might be in her class. Sabrina was also concerned about the little girl's well-being. She could handle a screaming teacher or a bully, but Daphne was only seven. This school might eat her alive.

Once she went through the cafeteria line, she searched the room for Daphne, fully expecting to find her huddled in a corner bawling her eyes out. Instead, she was stunned to find her sister sitting at a table packed with bright-eyed, happy kids, all hanging on her every word. As Sabrina approached, the children exploded with laughter when her sister pulled a ruler out of her big beehive hair.

"Daphne, you are the funniest person I have ever met!" one of her little friends said.

"What else do you have in there? Do it again!" another kid begged.

Daphne noticed her sister and smiled.

"Are you OK?" Sabrina asked.

"I'm having the time of my life."

"I need to tell you something," Sabrina said.

"Can it wait? I'm with my friends," Daphne said.

Friends? Of course Daphne would be popular. She was the hit of the second grade. Sabrina quietly envied her sister's charisma and trudged through the cafeteria looking for an empty table. Just as she was about to sit down, two kids quickly slipped into the seats as if she weren't there at all. She moved in the direction of another deserted table, but the same thing happened again. Sabrina was starting to wonder if she could eat standing up, when she felt her feet come out from under her. Her tray flew forward, sending her lunch splattering across the cafeteria. She slammed to the ground hard, pounding her chin into the cold floor, and saw little lights explode in front of her eyes.

Standing over her was Natalie. From below, the gigantic girl seemed apelike, with long, thick arms, a hulking body, and an underbite.

"Oops," the girl grunted in a low voice.

Toby, her tiny sidekick, stood nearby, giggling at Sabrina's misfortune.

"You did that on purpose," Sabrina said as she calmly got to her feet.

"What are you going to do about it, Grimm? Cry on me?" The big girl laughed.

"If you know my name, then you should know I don't cry," Sabrina said, clenching her fist tightly and socking the girl in the face. As the big goon fell backward, Sabrina's dreams of dull school days fell with her. When Sabrina turned to look around the cafeteria, the sleepy-faced kids from her class were now wide awake and gawking in wonder.

"I've met a lot of kids like you. You think you run this place," Sabrina said as she hovered over Natalie. "I'm sure you scare everyone, too, so they don't stand up to you. Just in case you still don't get it, you don't scare me."

"You shouldn't have done that," Toby hissed.

"That's exactly right!" a voice shouted, and a meaty hand grabbed Sabrina's arm. Before she could react, she felt herself being dragged away. Mr. Grumpner was pulling her toward the office. The vein in his forehead was throbbing.

"She started it!" Sabrina cried.

"And I'm ending it!" Grumpner shouted back.

Sabrina sat in Mr. Sheepshank's hot, windowless office waiting for her punishment. The mousy secretary with the thick glasses told her that the guidance counselor would be with her as soon as he was available. Three hours later, he still hadn't shown up, and Sabrina's temper was boiling over. She couldn't believe that with all the things wrong with this school she was being singled out for defending herself. Sixth grade was supposed to be about books and tests, not guerilla warfare. The kids were hateful. The teachers were despicable. It was just like being back in the orphanage.

By the time Mr. Sheepshank and his smiley-face bow tie showed up, Sabrina was seething. Mr. Grumpner followed him into the office, looking indignant, and the two men sat down.

"So, Sabrina," the counselor said, "do you want to tell us why Natalie is in the school infirmary with a black eye?"

"I'll tell you why!" Mr. Grumpner growled, nearly jumping out of his seat. "This one is trouble."

Mr. Sheepshank sat back in his chair and licked his lips as if he were preparing for a big meal. "Go on, Sabrina, what happened?"

"That ugly freak tripped me on purpose," Sabrina said, wiping the sweat from her brow.

"That's what she's saying," Grumpner interjected. "I saw the whole thing."

"If you'd seen the whole thing, then we wouldn't be sitting here!" Sabrina snapped, surprised by how quickly her anger overtook her. A headache was beginning to pound behind her eyes. She wondered if she were getting sick. All those nights of stakeouts must have finally worn down her defenses.

"Young lady, you have a bad attitude!" her teacher bellowed. "I don't know how school works in the big city, but in my classroom you will respect me or else!"

"Yeah, I've seen what 'or else' means in your classroom," the girl said. "I've seen how you teach children to respect you. You insult them, make fun of them, and drag them around. I dare you to try it on me! I just dare you!"

Mr. Grumpner backed away as if he had just stumbled upon a hornet's nest. "Are you going to let her talk to me like that?" he whined to the counselor.

"I believe that letting your feelings out is healthy," Mr. Sheepshank said. "Sabrina has a right to defend herself."

"Save your new-age psychobabble," the teacher grumbled. "What are you going to do to punish her?"

"Punish me?" Sabrina cried. "I didn't start the fight!"

"You can't go through the halls punching people in the eye."

"Mr. Grumpner, I think we need a breather," the counselor said as he rose from his chair. He crossed the room, took the grouchy teacher by the arm, and led him to the door. "If you spot any more slug-fests, please be sure to bring them to my attention immediately."

"You didn't tell me what you're going to do with her," Grumpner argued, but Mr. Sheepshank closed the door in his face.

The guidance counselor returned to his chair with a broad smile. "Interesting first day you are having," he said.

"I'm not going to let someone pick on me," Sabrina said.

"I'm not asking you to," Sheepshank replied. "I think Natalie got what she has had coming to her for a while. She's been pushing kids around since kindergarten. I bet it felt pretty good to knock her down. I heard a few children even applauded."

Sabrina was stunned. "Aren't you supposed to tell me that fighting isn't the answer?" she asked.

"Let's just pretend I did," Mr. Sheepshank continued with a wink. "Sabrina, I know being in the sixth grade isn't easy. There are lots of things that aren't fair, like bullies picking on you. It's a natural human emotion to get angry. So what are you supposed to do? Bottle it up? We all know what happens when you shake up a bottle of soda. It explodes all over the place. I think feelings are the same way. You've got to let them out when you're having them."

New-age psychobabble or not, Sabrina liked what Mr. Sheepshank was saying. Adults rarely understood her point of view, but

Mr. Sheepshank seemed sympathetic and eager to see her side of the problem. It was a bizarre feeling to have a grown-up understand her point of view, but she liked it a lot.

"I'm sure Grumpner would like to see you in detention, but I think we'll forget all about this," the counselor continued. "You've been sitting here for several hours and have had plenty of time to think about what happened."

Sabrina got up from her seat, then paused and asked, "Mr. Sheepshank, does it get any better?"

He laughed. "I wish I could say it does . . . But don't worry, someday this place will be nothing but an old memory."

Sabrina looked up at the clock. School had been over for five minutes. Daphne would be waiting.

"I have to go meet my sister."

"Of course," Mr. Sheepshank said.

"I'll see you tomorrow, then," she said.

"I'm on the edge of my seat," the guidance counselor replied.

Sabrina stepped into the hallway—and right into Natalie. The hulking girl was waiting by some lockers, her left eye black and purple with a bruise. When she spotted Sabrina, she turned and punched a locker door. The impact was so great, it dented the steel.

"See you around, Grimm," Natalie said, then pushed past her into Mr. Sheepshank's office.

Great, I've been here less than eight hours, and I already have a mortal enemy, Sabrina thought. *I wonder what Tuesday will be like?*

"Don't worry, Sabrina. Tomorrow's a new day," a voice behind her said. Sabrina spun around and found the pretty blond girl from her classes.

"That's what I'm worried about."

The girl laughed. "I'm Bella," she said. "And don't worry. Not everyone's like Natalie. Actually, no one's like Natalie. I think all those muscles make her dumb. Still, you might want to stay away from her for a while."

"I'll try," Sabrina said. "I'm Sabrina."

"Oh, I know who you are," Bella said. "That hair is sort of unforgettable."

Sabrina blushed and reached up to pat her hair down. She knew it wasn't making much of a difference.

"Don't worry," Natalie continued. "We all have bad hair days. One morning I forgot to wash the conditioner out of my hair. I looked like I'd been trapped in a rainstorm for three days."

Just then, Daphne rushed down the hallway to meet them.

"I've had the greatest day of my entire life!" she screamed as she hugged Sabrina tightly. "We spent the first part of the morning making papier-mâché hats, and then when the hats were dry, we put them on and learned about what kind of people might have worn them. I wore George Washington's hat."

"Daphne, this is Bella," Sabrina said, introducing the two. "She's in my homeroom."

"You made a friend?" Daphne asked, giving her sister another hug. "Oh, I'm so proud of you! Puck said you couldn't do it. In fact, he bet me you couldn't. I just won twenty bucks!"

"Cute kid," Bella said, giggling. "I gotta get going. See you tomorrow, slugger."

Sabrina nodded and watched the girl disappear down the hallway. Maybe there was a chance of having a normal friend, after all.

"Did you know that George Washington didn't really have wooden teeth? That's a myth. Ms. White said his teeth were made from ivory and bone, 'cause . . ." Daphne paused and looked around. Then she cupped her hand around her sister's ear and finished the sentence. ". . . she actually knew him. But she didn't tell the class that, just me."

"That's great, but I have something to tell you," Sabrina said.

Daphne waved her off, too excited by her stories to stop. "Then we learned all about chimpanzees. Did you know that chimpanzees aren't actually monkeys? I didn't know that. Chimpanzees are so punk rock."

"Punk rock?"

"You know, cool. Julie Melphy says it all the time, and she told me I could say it, too. Julie Melphy is very punk rock," her sister replied. "How was your day?"

"Horrible," Sabrina grumbled. "Come on, I need to get my coat from my locker, and there's something important you need to know about this school."

The girls climbed the steps as Sabrina told her sister about Mr. Hamelin and his son, Wendell.

Daphne was fascinated. "Does that make him half Everafter? Do you think his mom is an Everafter? I wonder who she is? Do you think there might be other Everafter kids here?" She had a million more questions before she was interrupted by Toby, who came running down the steps in their direction. He nearly knocked them over as he passed.

"Out of the way, lightning-bolt heads!" he shouted, then laughed his annoying little laugh as he disappeared down the hall.

That kid is so un-punk rock, Sabrina thought.

The sisters reached Sabrina's locker, and she went to work on the combination. She pointed out Mr. Grumpner's class across the hall and explained how mean he was to the students.

"What kind of class are you in?" Daphne asked as she peered through the window into Grumpner's room.

"What are you talking about?" Sabrina asked as she put on her coat.

"You need to see this," her sister said.

Sabrina closed her locker and gazed through the window. The room was a disaster. It looked as if a tornado had gone through it. Desks and chairs were tossed around, and an odd white substance covered everything. She opened the door, and she and Daphne stepped inside to find the window shattered and cold air blasting into the room. It caused the white substance to flutter around, like strands of silky ribbons. In the center of the room, hanging from the ceiling, was a sac made out of the substance. It was huge and slowly swaying in the wind.

"What is this?" Daphne asked, poking at the sac.

"Don't touch anything," Sabrina said, removing a strand attached to her coat. She grabbed a nearby chair, pulled it close to the sac, and climbed onto the seat. Once she had her balance, she peered closely at the substance. She could see something inside but couldn't make out what it was.

"Look at this," Daphne said, bending down beneath the window. There she found several black feathers littering the floor. She gestured around the room to more of them. "Where did they all come from?"

"Something's inside this sac," Sabrina said, returning her attention to the strange substance. She pulled off layer after layer until she began to reveal something buried deep inside. The more she uncovered, the more she understood that what was inside the sac was not a thing but a person.

"It's Mr. Grumpner," she whispered. The old man was as purple as an eggplant, and his once-puffy face was gaunt and drained. "He's dead."

"Aww, man! That's so gross!" Daphne cried, upset.

"Who could have done this?" Sabrina wondered.

"Probably whoever left that," the little girl said, pointing at the front of the classroom.

Sabrina turned to see what her sister was referring to. On the chalkboard was another horrible but familiar sight. Someone had dipped his or her hand into a can of paint and pressed it on the wall. The handprint was bright red. It was the mark of the Scarlet Hand.

4

THE SCHOOL DOORS FLEW OPEN, AND A DARK-haired man in a purple suit strutted in with his nose in the air. When Sabrina spotted him, she groaned. Mayor William Charming was not one of her favorite people, despite the fact that he was really Prince Charming, the dashing romantic hero of a dozen fairy tales. But, as Sabrina knew firsthand, he was Charming only in name. The mayor could be an obnoxious, rude know-it-all, and he had a particular disdain for Sabrina's family.

Racing beside him was Mr. Seven, the mayor's diminutive sidekick. Seven was actually one of the seven dwarfs and acted as Charming's driver, assistant, and whipping boy. Behind him was Sheriff Hamstead, who did his best to keep pace with the others while trying to hoist his pants up.

"So let's go through this one more time," the mayor said con-descendingly. "Who's doing all the talking?"

"You are," Hamstead and Mr. Seven said in unison.

"And why is that?"

"Because we are numbskulls."

"See how easy that was?"

"But what if I see something suspicious? I am the sheriff, after all," Hamstead argued.

Charming came to a halt and spun around on his heels. "Are you going to make me get out the idiot hat? 'Cause it sounds to me like someone wants to wear the idiot hat!"

The sheriff frowned and shook his head.

"Good," Mayor Charming snapped. He took a deep breath and closed his eyes. "OK, let's relax. Let out all the anger and frustration. You are a great mayor. Smile."

Suddenly, a smile sprang to Charming's face, and he started down the hallway again. The mayor was a master at the phony, toothy grin, but it slid off his face when he spotted Sabrina and Daphne.

"What are they doing here?" he moaned.

"The girls found the body," the sheriff explained.

"The sisters Grimm found the body . . . and no one told me?" Charming said.

"You told us not to talk," Mr. Seven said defensively.

The mayor bit down on his lower lip and mumbled a variety of curse words Sabrina had never heard before. He reached into his pocket, took out a folded piece of paper, and handed it to Mr. Seven, who looked down at it and frowned. The dwarf unfolded it, revealing a pointy paper hat, and put it on his head. Someone had written I AM AN IDIOT in big black letters on the front of it. Mr. Seven lowered his eyes in humiliation.

"Howdy, Mayor," Daphne said happily. Even though Charming considered the Grimms his eternal enemies, Daphne had a soft spot for him. Recently, the mayor had helped the family stop Jack the Giant Killer's plan to let giants loose on the town, and, most important, Charming had been kind to Elvis when the big dog was injured. The little girl was now convinced that deep down Mayor Charming was one of the good guys.

"Sheriff, let's make a new law. Meddling children go to jail," he said through gritted teeth.

"You're so funny," Daphne said, smiling into the mayor's face. The little girl grabbed his necktie, yanked him down to her level, and gave him a smooch on the nose. The anger melted from his face, only to be replaced by confusion. He pulled away like he had accidentally touched a hot stove, then straightened his clothes.

Just then, Principal Hamelin rushed down the hall to join them. "Mayor Charming, Sheriff Hamstead—thank goodness you are here. This is such a terrible tragedy. I want you two to know that I will cooperate in any way I can. I feel horrible this happened at our school."

"I appreciate that, Piper," Charming said, shaking the man's hand. "We'll get to the bottom of this and be out of your hair as soon as possible. I assume you don't have any more of these running around the building?" He waved his hand at the girls as if he were trying to shoo away a couple of annoying houseflies.

"You mean children?" the principal said. "Oh, no. The body was discovered at the end of the day. Most of the children were already on their way home."

"Sheriff, let's take a look," Charming said, gesturing to the door of Mr. Grumpner's classroom.

Charming and Hamstead stepped forward, trying to enter the room at the same time, and got jammed in the doorway together. They squirmed and shoved but were trapped until Mr. Seven came up from behind and pushed them into the room.

"I thought we weren't going to do that anymore," Mr. Charming said, maintaining his phony smile in front of everyone.

Hamstead muttered an apology as he took a camera from his pocket. He snapped pictures of the unusual crime scene and Mr. Grumpner's disturbing corpse, paying close attention to the red handprint on the blackboard.

"When was the victim discovered?" Hamstead asked.

"About ten minutes after the last bell," Sabrina offered.

"I see," said Hamstead. He stepped close to the body still suspended in the sticky sac and took more photos. He pulled aside a strand of the white substance to get a better look at Mr. Grumpner's face. "Looks like he's been completely drained of blood."

"Maybe it was a vampire!" Daphne cried.

"There's no such thing as vampires," Charming muttered.

I used to think there was no such thing as you, Sabrina thought.

"Sheriff, do you have any idea what happened to him?" the principal asked.

"Well," Hamstead said as he put his camera away, "if I had to hazard a guess, I'd say—"

"Spiders," Charming interrupted. "A whole bunch of spiders did this to him. It's a freak accident, but nothing supernatural or magical, for sure. There are so many cobwebs here, I'd say it took hundreds of spiders to make them. They must have come through that open window over there."

"It's too cold for spiders," the sheriff argued, but when the mayor flashed him an angry look, the portly policeman zipped his lips.

"Murdered by spiders?" Sabrina asked. "What would you say their motivation was to kill my teacher?"

Sabrina's sarcasm was lost on the mayor. "How should I know?"

"Maybe Mr. Grumpner stepped on one, and its family wanted revenge," Hamstead said, clearly trying to help his boss's theory sound less ridiculous.

"Spider revenge?" Sabrina asked.

"I suppose you have a better theory," Charming snapped.

Suddenly, the door opened, and Granny Relda and Mr. Canis entered the room.

"Oh, I have a theory," Granny Relda said, scanning the room. "It was a monster."

Daphne ran to the old woman and wrapped her arms around her.

"We found something gross!" the little girl cried, burying her face in the old woman's bright green dress. Granny bent down and kissed her on the forehead, then crossed the room to Sabrina and took her by the hand.

"Are you OK, *liebling*?"

Sabrina nodded, though she wasn't sure it was true. She wasn't sure exactly how to feel. If she had to describe it, she might say that she felt numb.

"A monster!" Charming laughed. "You've had some insane theories in the past, Relda, but a monster?"

"You're right, Mayor," Mr. Canis said sarcastically. "Ferryport Landing has fairies, witches, robots, and men made out of straw, but monsters? Now she's really lost her marbles!"

"Relda, I believe there's a law in this town about keeping animals on a leash," Charming said.

Mr. Canis let out a low growl. The men stared at each other for a long moment, until Charming composed himself.

"This has nothing to do with the Everafter community, Canis. No one in this town would murder a human."

"No one is that stupid," Hamelin said.

"Well, it appears someone clearly is that stupid," Granny Relda said. "Daphne, what do you have in your hand?"

The little girl held up one of the black feathers she had noticed just moments earlier. "We found a clue."

"Excellent detective work, girls," the old woman said.

Daphne beamed with pride.

Sheriff Hamstead took the feather and eyed it closely. "Looks like crow to me," he said. "There're a couple more there under the windowsill."

Mr. Canis took a deep sniff of the air. "It is crow."

"It probably blew in with the wind," Charming said, snatching the feather from the sheriff's pudgy hand. He tossed it to the floor as if it were meaningless.

Granny scooped it up and placed it in her handbag, then jotted something in her notebook.

"And then there's that!" Daphne said, pointing to the hand-print.

Hamstead, Charming, Mr. Seven, and Principal Hamelin all peered at the red symbol closely. Each of them wore a worried expression.

"It's just like the one the police found in my parents' abandoned car," Sabrina said.

"And the one on Jack's shirt when he attacked us in the woods," Daphne said.

"Or maybe that blew in with the wind, too," Canis said.

Charming scowled. "It's probably just a prank."

"A prank?" Sabrina and Daphne cried in disbelief.

"Mayor Charming, that's the sign of the Scarlet Hand," said Granny Relda.

"There's no such thing as the Scarlet Hand," he said. "Hamstead has done a thorough investigation, and we've concluded that Jack invented the whole thing."

Sabrina was stunned. Charming knew the Scarlet Hand was real. He'd admitted to the girls that the shadowy group had approached him. Why was he lying about its existence? Before she could confront him, the door opened, and Snow White entered. It shouldn't have been possible, but Ms. White seemed to get more beautiful every time Sabrina saw her.

Charming rushed to block her view of Mr. Grumpner's corpse, but Ms. White had already spotted it.

"Snow, you shouldn't see this," Charming said softly.

"So it's true," she gasped.

Charming took Ms. White by the hand and led her into the hallway. Sabrina and Daphne shared a glance and pushed through the crowd, eager not to miss a second of this royal soap opera.

"Billy," Ms. White said, "what did that to him?"

"Try to put it out of your head, Snow," he said. He put his hand on her shoulder and looked deep into her eyes. It was hard to believe that the usually obnoxious mayor could be so tender. "We'll find out who did this. I've got my best men on it."

Everyone filed out of Grumpner's classroom. Sheriff Hamstead took a roll of yellow police tape from his jacket and draped an X over the door to keep anyone else from entering.

Ms. White bent down so that she was at eye level with Daphne. "Are you OK?" she asked.

"Don't worry about me," the little girl answered. "We see this kind of thing all the time. It goes with the job."

Mayor Charming turned to the sheriff. "Mr. Hamstead, could you make sure my fiancée . . . I mean, Ms. White, gets home safely?" he said, reddening over his mistake.

The bright blush on Snow's cheeks flashed like a police siren on her pale skin.

"I'd be happy to," Sheriff Hamstead said, extending his arm to the beautiful woman. He escorted her down the hall, but not before she stopped to gaze back at Charming.

"So what's next, Mayor?" Principal Hamelin asked.

"Don't you mean Billy?" Sabrina asked, before she burst into giggles. Daphne and Granny Relda joined her. Even Mr. Canis cracked a smile. Suddenly, a loud, goofy laugh was heard behind them. When they turned, they found Mr. Seven bent over with glee. "That's just precious. It's so sweet, I'm going to get a cavity."

"Don't tease him. I think it's romantic," Daphne said, doing her best to stop laughing.

"Enough!" Charming shouted, silencing everyone's giggles. "This is a crime scene. Relda, take your brats and your mangy mongrel with you, or I'll have you arrested."

"Watch your words, Prince," Canis growled as his eyes turned icy blue, showing everyone that the Wolf was just below the surface. "Someday you're going to wake up and find someone has taken a bite out of you."

"That's quite enough," Granny said, stepping between the two men. Every time Charming and Canis were in a room together, they were at each other's throats, but the old woman had a way of making them feel foolish. They stepped back and lowered their eyes like two squabbling schoolboys. "It's time to go."

Hamelin walked the family to the door.

"Relda, I really appreciate your interest in this, but I do think a murder investigation is a job for the police, don't you?" he said. "I'd prefer to keep this terrible tragedy as quiet as possible."

"We'll do our best to stay out of the way, Mr. Hamelin," Granny said, then suddenly bent to run a finger along the floor. She stood and stared at it closely. It was filthy with chalky white dust. "I think your custodian might be sleeping on the job. This place could use a good mopping."

Hamelin looked down at the floor. "Yes, I think you're right."

The family found their ancient black jalopy in the parking lot. The beat-up monstrosity was in desperate need of a tune-up, and its long-neglected shocks groaned and complained as everyone climbed into their seats. Elvis was in the back, snuggling under a huge blanket, and didn't even bother to lift his head when the family arrived. Daphne wrapped her arms around the dog's neck and gave him a big wet smooch on the forehead.

"I missed you today," she announced.

Elvis tucked his head under his blanket and hid.

"What's the matter with him?" the little girl asked.

"He's pouting. He doesn't like to be left in the car," Granny Relda said as she jotted something in her notebook.

"Aww, my little baby," Daphne said, trying to pull the two-hundred-pound dog onto her lap like an infant. She showered the Great Dane in kisses. "Is somebody sad? Did somebody get left in the car? I won't ever leave you in the car."

Elvis gave the girl a lick on the cheek, and she giggled.

Granny spun around in her seat with a delighted look on her face. "*Lieblings*, you know what all this means?"

Sabrina groaned. "We're in the middle of a mystery?"

"Isn't it exciting?" the old woman cried.

"Yes, and a distraction," Sabrina argued. "You heard Charming and his ridiculous spider theory. He knows the Scarlet Hand killed Mr. Grumpner, but instead he lies about it. Grumpner was a human, so Charming couldn't care less. Why should the Everafter mayor and the Everafter police department do anything at all? No, they'll just cover up his death, and we'll run into one dead end after another. Shouldn't we focus more attention on Mom and Dad?"

"We are Grimms, and this is what we do," Daphne said.

"Exactly right, little one. We are Grimms, and part of what we do is make sure that this kind of thing doesn't get swept under the rug. Sabrina, I assure you that nearly all of my energy is spent trying to locate Henry and Veronica, but we can't shirk our other responsibilities."

Suddenly, Mr. Seven was tapping on the car window. He motioned for Granny Relda to roll it down as he looked around nervously.

"Good evening, Mr. Seven."

"Mayor Charming has requested your presence at the mansion. He has something he wishes to discuss in private."

Granny Relda and Mr. Canis shared a suspicious glance. After a moment, Mr. Canis nodded his approval.

"Tell Mr. Charming we'll be there," the old woman said.

The dwarf nodded and walked over to the mayor's long white limousine. He buffed the silver stallion on the hood with his shirt-sleeve, then climbed onto the stack of phone books on the driver's seat. Soon the limo was pulling onto the road.

"Are you sure you're feeling up to this?" Granny asked, putting her hand on Mr. Canis's shoulder. The old man nodded. He started the car, and it sputtered to life with a series of backfires that Sabrina was sure could be heard in the next town.

They followed Charming's limo through the quiet country roads of Ferryport Landing until they pulled into the sprawling mayoral estate. Mr. Canis parked the car and turned off the engine. The last time Sabrina had been at the mansion, it was lit up like a Christmas tree for the Ferryport Landing Fund-raising Ball, an annual event during which the Everafter community came together to be themselves, celebrate, and donate to Charming's "town fund." Without all the glitz and glamour, Charming's mansion looked vacant. The lights were off, and the fountain, which featured a lifelike sculpture of Charming, was drained and full of dead leaves.

"Mrs. Grimm, if it's OK with you, I believe I will stay here," Mr. Canis said as he opened the car door for Granny Relda. "I'm feeling a bit tired, and I suspect Charming will only make it worse."

"Of course, Mr. Canis," Granny Relda said. "I don't believe Mayor Charming poses any threat to us."

Elvis whined when he saw that the family was leaving him in the car again.

"Elvis, we're not leaving you in the car. We're putting you in charge of it," Daphne said. The dog lifted his huge ears as if he was listening very carefully. "It's a really important job. You have to stay and guard Mr. Canis. Don't let anything bad happen to him."

Elvis barked, confirming his orders. He sat up in the backseat and watched out the windows for any would-be attackers.

As the Grimms approached the mansion, Sabrina looked back and noticed Canis doing something very odd. The stick-thin man had climbed on top of the car and was sitting cross-legged on the roof. He closed his eyes and rested his hands on his knees.

"What's he doing?" Sabrina asked.

"Meditating," Granny replied, as if this were the natural response. "It helps him remain centered and calm."

Of course the Big Bad Wolf meditates, Sabrina thought. *Why did I even bother to ask?*

The trio stood on the front steps, but before Granny could ring the bell, Mr. Seven opened the door and ushered them into the house. Sabrina noticed right away that the mansion was filthy. Several curtains in the ballroom had fallen and lay in heaps on the floor. A giant red stain had ruined a polar bear rug lying near the fireplace. The carpet on the stairs needed a good vacuuming, and a bucket sat on the floor collecting rain from a giant patched-up hole in the ceiling. Half a dozen overflowing bags of garbage sat by the door waiting to be taken out, and a thick layer of dust covered everything, including a full suit of armor that leaned precariously against a wall.

"Good evening," Mr. Seven said, and, without offering to take their coats, he turned and raced up the staircase. "I'll get the mayor."

"What do you think he wants?" Daphne wondered.

"Hard to say," Granny Relda said. "The mayor is full of surprises."

"Maybe he felt like he didn't get to insult us enough at the school," Sabrina muttered just as Charming appeared at the top of the steps. Sabrina watched him take a deep breath before he came down to join them.

"What happened here?" Sabrina asked, gesturing to the mess.

"You happened here!" Charming snapped. "You and your smelly sister ruined the only fund-raising event this town has each year."

Daphne raised an arm to smell her armpit. She crinkled her nose and lowered her arm quickly. "I'm not that bad," she said.

"You crashed an invitation-only party and brought a giant here, which nearly destroyed the mansion and several cars in the parking lot. Worst of all, you made me look like a fool in front of the town's biggest donors," the mayor said. "We didn't raise a penny. The town is broke."

"We know what the fund-raiser is really for," Sabrina replied. "You want to buy everything and turn Ferryport Landing into your personal kingdom. Why don't you just dip into the money you've conned out of everyone for the last two hundred years?"

Charming growled. "I haven't taken a penny out of this town. The rumors about my finances are greatly exaggerated. Relda, do you believe I would live in this cramped shack if I didn't have to?

"Services had to be cut drastically," he continued. "Transportation, education—I was even forced to fire the statue polishers. Poor Mr. Seven has agreed to a substantial cut in pay, and I haven't taken a salary in weeks. I had to lay off three-fourths of the town's police force, which, since there were only four police officers to begin with, leaves me with one pig."

"That must be challenging," Granny Relda said, "but I'm sure you didn't ask us here for a donation."

"No, I didn't. This conversation must be an absolute secret," he said as he leaned down and pinned a shiny tin star onto Sabrina's coat. It looked like the kind sheriffs wore in old black-and-white Western movies. She peered down at it and read the words FERRY-PORT LANDING SPECIAL FORCES DEPUTY OFFICER.

"What's this?" she asked.

"I'm deputizing you," he said as he pinned a similar star onto Daphne's coat.

The little girl looked at it and beamed. "Look at me! I'm a cowboy!"

"I don't think I understand what is taking place, Mayor," Granny Relda said.

"May I?" Charming asked Granny Relda. The old woman hesitated but finally agreed, and he pinned a star onto her coat, too. "Working Ernest to death is not in my best interest, and since there appears to be a murderer running free, I am forced to do what is in the best interest of the town and recruit citizens with investigative skills. Raise your right hand and repeat after me."

"Wait—you're making us police officers?" Sabrina cried.

"Undercover police officers, and only temporarily," he said. "Once the teacher's killer has been captured, you will be expected to turn in your badges."

Charming raised his right hand and waited for the Grimms to do the same.

Sabrina stared blankly at the man, wondering if maybe he was pulling some kind of prank on them.

"Don't make this harder on me than it has to be," he begged. "Do you think I would ask you if it wasn't absolutely necessary? I swore I'd see your family rot before I asked for your help, but drastic times call for drastic measures. The Scarlet Hand must be stopped."

"So now the Scarlet Hand exists, huh? Why did you lie about it back at the school?" Sabrina asked.

"Because I don't need the citizens of this town to panic. If word got out that there was a terrorist group killing people, there would be chaos in the streets. Hamstead can barely keep up now with speeding tickets and jaywalkers," Charming continued. "If you don't stop whatever did that to Mr. Grumpner, then it won't get stopped."

"Why do you care what happens to a human teacher?" Sabrina asked. "I thought you hated humans."

"Sabrina, you're being rude," Granny scolded. "I'm sure the mayor is not so coldhearted."

"You don't want anything bad to happen to Ms. White," Daphne said to Charming. "You're in love with her. You want to kiss and hug her! You want to write her love notes. You want to hold her hand in the park and look at puppies in the pet store."

"Is there an off button for this one?" Charming asked Granny Relda.

The old woman grinned at the mayor. "You're not denying it, Mr. Mayor."

"All right!" Charming surrendered. "Snow has a knack for getting into trouble. I would sleep better at night knowing she is safe."

"Does she know you got the feels for her?" Daphne asked.

Charming lowered his eyes. "It's complicated," he said, then turned red with anger. "Why am I talking to you about this? Will you help me or not?"

"Of course we'll do what we can," Granny Relda assured him.

"What are you going to do for us?" Sabrina asked.

The old woman looked at the girl in horror. "*Liebling*, we would never take payment for helping folks."

"Granny, finding the killer is going to take a lot of time—time that we could be using to find Mom and Dad," Sabrina argued.

"What can I do?" Charming asked.

"You have connections we don't," said Sabrina. "People will talk to you. Maybe someone knows something. Maybe you have something magical lying around we could use to help find our parents. Use your imagination, Billy."

Charming nodded, then raised his right hand. "Repeat after me. I do solemnly swear to protect and serve the inhabitants of—"

"What does *inhabitants* mean?" Daphne interrupted.

"It means the people who live in a particular place," her sister answered, noting Charming's impatient face.

"Why didn't you just say *the people*, then?" the little girl asked.

"Let him finish, *lieblings*," Granny Relda said.

"I do solemnly swear," Charming started over, "to protect and serve the people of Ferryport Landing to the best of my ability. I vow to protect the peace, secure the safety of the town, and uphold the rule of law."

The Grimms repeated what he said, word for word, and then lowered their hands.

"You are now officially deputized under the laws of Ferryport

Landing," the mayor said as he pulled out a set of keys and handed them to Granny Relda.

"What are these?" Granny asked, looking down at the key ring.

"Keys to the school," Charming said. "You'll need them to get inside."

Granny smiled and handed the keys back to the mayor. "I've got my own set, thanks," she said.

Charming scowled and shoved the keys back into his pocket. "Well, I'd love to keep this happy event going all night, but as you know, I can't stand you people," he said, leading them to the door. As his hand clutched the knob, he turned and looked the girls in their eyes. "Snow is important to me. I would appreciate you keeping a close eye on her."

"No problem, Billy," Daphne replied, wrapping her arms around the mayor and hugging him tightly. "It's sooooo romantic!"

Charming sneered, opened the door, and forcefully shoved the family outside.

"You should really tell her that you love her," Daphne said, right before the mayor slammed the door in her face.

Sabrina had been to a lot of schools in the past year and a half, and they all had a few things in common: grouchy teachers, a bully, a bully's punching bag, a weird cafeteria lady, a bathroom that everyone was afraid to go into, and a librarian who worshiped something called the Dewey Decimal System. None of those schools, however, had a teacher-killing monster scurrying through its hallways.

Granny Relda was convinced that a monster—maybe working with the Scarlet Hand—had killed Mr. Grumpner. With their shiny new police badges still pinned to their chests, the old woman and the girls went back to the school to do some more snooping. Not knowing exactly what the monster looked like or where it might be now was doing a number on Sabrina's nerves as she crept through the darkened hallways with Daphne and Granny Relda. The long shadows cast by the setting sun looked like dinosaurs and invading aliens. Every little creak sounded like an approaching Bigfoot or a swamp monster. And worse, Grumpner's bloodless purple face appeared every time Sabrina closed her eyes. All she wanted to do was run back to the car and hide under Elvis's blanket, but Granny was insistent. She was convinced there were clues they had missed earlier and that the crime scene needed a second look. For once, Sabrina wished Mr. Canis was by their side, but the skinny old man was back on the roof of the car meditating in the freezing cold. Luckily, Elvis had come along this time.

"Mr. Canis looks terrible—and for him, that's particularly bad," Sabrina said as she peered through a window into an empty classroom.

"Yes, the fight with Jack caused him some setbacks. In the past he has always been able to tap into the Wolf's strengths without losing control," her grandmother explained, "but this time he tasted Jack's blood, and it strengthened his big bad alter ego. Don't worry, children. Mr. Canis will win this battle, as he has in the past."

"But what if he doesn't?" Sabrina asked.

"Trust that your grandmother has a plan for every possibility."

And do you have a plan for making sure we don't end up in the Wolf's belly? Sabrina wondered.

When they arrived at Sabrina's homeroom, the crime scene tape and Grumpner's body were both gone. The broken window was repaired, and all the cobwebs were cleared away. Even the bloodred hand painted on the chalkboard was washed clean. Other than a few misplaced chairs, there was no evidence of the gruesome scene they'd witnessed only hours before. Sabrina wondered if Hamelin was responsible for cleaning the place up, or if Charming had sent one of the Three to magically put things back to normal.

"They've cleaned the room, Granny. If there were more clues, they're all gone now," Daphne said.

The old woman took out her notebook and jotted a few words with a stubby pencil. "I believe the room may reveal a few details yet. First of all, I don't believe Mr. Grumpner was taken unawares. The way these chairs are scattered, it looks like he tried to fight back."

Sabrina shuddered as she imagined her teacher fighting off his attacker. Whether it was a giant spider or a thousand little ones, the fact was that the man's death had been horrible. Even a grouch like Grumpner didn't deserve to die so painfully.

Granny crossed the room and opened Grumpner's desk drawers. They were empty except for the bottom one. Inside was a picture of him and a woman. They were on a boat, enjoying an afternoon on the Hudson River. Grumpner and the woman held glasses of champagne and were toasting each other.

"His wife?" Sabrina asked as Granny showed her the picture. "I can't imagine Mr. Cranky found someone to marry him."

"He was probably a very different man at home," the old woman replied. "You told me once you thought your father was too careful, but the Henry Grimm I know threw caution to the wind. There are many sides to us all."

"His wife must be very sad." Daphne sighed.

"I suppose so," Granny replied. "It's very hard to lose someone you love."

"Well, we found a picture," Sabrina said, eyeing a shadow in the corner that looked a lot like the bogeyman. "Can we go now? This place is giving me the willies."

"Don't you be afraid, ma'am," Daphne said. "I'm a police officer. I'm here to protect you." She hitched up her belt, then walked around the room mimicking Sheriff Hamstead's bowlegged gait.

Sabrina laughed so hard that she snorted.

Granny reached into her handbag and pulled out a familiar pair of infrared goggles. "Just a few more moments," she said as she put the goggles over her eyes and looked around the room, finally focusing on the floor. "Aha! Children, come and take a look."

The girls hurried to their grandmother. Daphne took the goggles and looked down at the floor. "That is so punk rock!" she said.

Eager for a turn, Sabrina snatched the goggles away from her sister and peered through their special lenses. They revealed ghostly white footprints—the last traces of the late Mr. Grumpner.

Granny Relda reached down and ran her finger across the floor. When she lifted it, there was white powder on it. "The plot thickens," she said, holding her chalky finger up to Sabrina's eyes. "This school is unusually dusty. Luckily, it's leaving behind a nice set of footprints to follow."

"They're coming from out in the hallway," Sabrina said, opening the door and following the glowing footprints.

"Notice anything about the steps?" her grandmother asked, following closely behind.

"They're very far apart," Sabrina said. "Three of my steps equal one of his."

"That's because he was running," the old woman informed her.

Sabrina was impressed. Granny Relda was a natural detective, and Sabrina wondered if she'd ever be as smart.

She led the family down the hall, following each step. She could see them leading around a corner, so she led the group in that direction until the infrared goggles were suddenly snatched off her head.

"Hey!" she complained as she turned on her little sister. "If you wanted to wear them, all you had to do was ask!"

Granny and Daphne said nothing. They were looking up at the ceiling with odd expressions on their faces. Sabrina followed their gaze until a shock rushed down to her toes. Hanging upside down above them was a fat, frog-faced creature. Its head and feet were amphibious, with slimy, bumpy skin and a puffed, bulbous pouch under its lower lip, yet it had the arms, legs, and torso of a human being. A long tongue spilled out of its mouth with the goggles sticking to the end. It dragged them into its mouth, but when it realized they couldn't be eaten, it spit them out at Sabrina's feet, spraying gooey saliva all over the girl's pants.

"Um, no thanks. You can keep them," Sabrina said.

The frog monster let out an odd, feminine giggle and puffed up its huge air sac. Sabrina had seen frogs do just the same thing on TV. She remembered they did it when they were preparing to eat. Something told her she and her family were on the menu.

"Run!" she cried.

The Grimms and Elvis ran down the hallway until the monster leaped off the ceiling and landed in front of them, blocking their path.

"I spy with my little eye," the frog-girl gurgled, "something yummy."

5

RANNY RELDA SWUNG HER HANDBAG AT THE
frog-girl and cracked her on her forehead. The monster groaned and fell to the ground. Sabrina knew
the sort of stuff the old woman kept in her purse—everything
from spy goggles to rolls of quarters. It packed quite a wallop.
So she was surprised when the frog-girl stirred, then struggled
to stand.

Not wasting any time, the Grimms spun in the opposite direction and raced down the stairs. Elvis followed close behind,
clumsily navigating the steep steps and barking threateningly.

"If we're lucky," Granny Relda said through winded breaths,
"that creature will be too afraid of Elvis to come after us."

"And if we aren't?" Sabrina asked as she helped her grandmother
down the last of the steps. Unfortunately, Sabrina's worries came
true. The frog-girl bounced down the steps and onto a nearby
wall, sticking like a suction cup.

"Your puppy isn't very nice," the frog-girl croaked. "But he'll digest in my belly as quickly as the three of you."

Daphne stepped forward and flashed her shiny new deputy's badge. "You're under arrest for . . . for . . . being gross!" she stammered, but the frog-girl was not impressed. She lunged for the little girl, but Sabrina grabbed Daphne's hand and dragged her down the hallway toward the exit. The monster gave chase, leaping from wall to wall, gaining ground with each jump so that by the time the Grimms reached the exit, the frog-girl was breathing down their necks. She shot her thick tongue out and wrapped it around Daphne's arm, dragging the little girl back into her clutches.

Elvis snapped viciously at the creature, but she jumped to the ceiling and hung upside down out of his reach.

"Let her go!" Sabrina shouted.

The frog-girl let out a sickening giggle and continued to dangle Daphne right out of Sabrina's reach. The little girl struggled and squirmed, then finally reached into her beehive hairdo and yanked the protractor she kept there out of her sticky locks. She stabbed the frog's tongue with its pointy tip, and the monster shrieked, releasing her. Daphne landed hard and knocked Sabrina to the ground.

"And you didn't like my hairdo," Daphne said to her sister. Sabrina quickly helped the little girl to her feet, and the two ran to the exit doors, with Granny Relda and Elvis close behind. They pushed the doors open and ran into the chilly air, making a beeline for the parking lot.

"Start the car!" Sabrina shouted as they sprinted across the school lawn. Mr. Canis, who was still meditating on top of the car, opened his eyes and, without pausing, climbed off the roof. Within seconds he had the old jalopy roaring. The sound of metal grinding on metal filled the air, and the machine shook violently. The old junker's obnoxious concert had never sounded so good to Sabrina.

"I assume there is a problem?" Mr. Canis said as Elvis, Granny, and the girls clambered into the car. No one got a chance to explain. Something slammed onto the roof. It was so loud, they all jumped—except Mr. Canis, whose only reaction was to look up and raise a questioning eyebrow. A slimy green hand smacked the driver's-side window, and Sabrina and Daphne screamed. Granny Relda whooped in astonishment, and Elvis growled and bared his teeth. Mr. Canis, however, took a deep breath, put the car into drive, and stomped on the gas. The tires squealed, and the car rocketed into the street, skidding across the country road before some quick steering set it straight.

"So it appears your monster theory was correct," Mr. Canis said as the creature pounded on the roof.

"Indeed. Though I'd like to amend my theory by saying that there is more than one monster involved," Granny Relda said. "Old friend, I think our passenger on the roof might be a little difficult to shake. Perhaps I should drive."

"You know very well the police took your license away," Mr. Canis said, steering from one side of the road to the other in an effort to dislodge their stowaway. Unfortunately, nothing the old man did had any effect on the monster, and she continued to beat violently on the roof.

"They completely overreacted, Mr. Canis. It was just a couple of speeding tickets," Granny said defensively.

"You were arrested fourteen times for reckless endangerment. Several neighborhood groups banned you from driving on their streets. Basil told me the German government passed a law in Berlin that says if you are ever caught in a car in their city, you will be hanged," the old man corrected.

"Oh, Mr. Canis," Granny begged, "no one has to know."

He shook his head.

"Please?"

Mr. Canis slammed on the brake pedal, and the car screeched to a halt. The frog-girl tumbled down the hood and bounced along the road for several yards. She let out a terrible moan, then lay still.

"You have to stay off major roads," the old man said.

Granny squealed with delight.

Mr. Canis got out of the car and walked around to the passenger side while Granny scooted over into the driver's seat. As they switched places, Sabrina watched the grotesque frog-girl stir, slowly get to her feet, and stare at the car. Even with her bizarre, twisted face, the murderous rage in her eyes was clear.

"Um, is this the best time to change drivers?" Sabrina asked.

"Children," Mr. Canis said as he turned to face the sisters, "put on your seat belts, and if you have any final words for your maker, I suggest you pray."

The girls eyed each other nervously. Unfortunately, the ancient seat belts installed in the car were torn, so Mr. Canis used ropes to improvise. Sabrina helped Daphne tie hers into a knot around her waist and then went to work on her own while Granny revved the engine and giggled.

"I feel so alive," the old woman said.

The frog-girl leaped into the air and came down violently on the car's front end. The impact was so great, the car's back end lifted a full four feet off the ground, then came down hard. The monster leaned forward to get a better look through the windshield and then licked her wide lips.

"Going somewhere?" She laughed.

"I almost feel sorry for the ugly thing," Mr. Canis said with a sigh.

Granny floored the accelerator, and the car lunged forward. The monster tumbled over the hood, up the windshield, over the roof and onto the trunk, and fell off the back end of the car.

"She's gone!" Sabrina cried as she watched the creature disappear behind them, but no sooner had she stopped cheering than the freak hopped back onto the trunk.

"She's back!" Daphne shouted, diving under the blanket with Elvis.

Granny made a sharp left onto an old dirt road and pressed hard on the gas pedal. The ancient car screamed in protest but jumped ahead with a burst of speed so powerful, Sabrina felt the g-force pushing her body into the seat springs. Granny's steering left a lot to be desired. She plowed through shrubbery, downed a picket fence, and smashed four mailboxes without even flinching.

"Perhaps you might like to stay on the road?" Mr. Canis shouted over the noise.

"This is so much fun!" Granny Relda cheered.

Despite the incredible speed and the flying debris, the frog-girl held on with little effort and pounded angrily on the rear window. Her massive blows created a thick crack in the glass. It wouldn't hold for much longer.

"Turning right!" Granny shouted from the driver's seat, just before she made an impossibly sharp turn. Elvis tumbled over the girls as the car banked. But the maneuver didn't seem to shake the monster.

"Turning left!" Granny shouted, and Elvis tumbled to the other side of the car, landing heavily on Sabrina's belly and knocking the wind out of her.

The frog-girl smacked the window again, and this time it exploded, sending chunks of glass into the backseat. Several large portions of the window stayed attached, but the monster pulled them off effortlessly and tossed them into the road. Then she reached into the backseat with her big sticky hands, unfastened Daphne's rope belt, and snatched the little girl right out of her seat. Sabrina grabbed desperately at Daphne's ankle and tried to pull her back inside the car, but the monster's grip was too strong.

Mr. Canis sprang into action. He rolled down his window and pulled his upper body out of the speeding car.

"There's no need to hurry, old man," the frog-girl screamed over the wind. "You'll die soon enough."

A ferocious roar echoed back at the monster, and Sabrina could see her eyes grow wide with surprise.

"You're the traitor!" the frog-girl cried. "I've heard of you. The Big Bad Wolf—trying to make amends for all the bad things you've done. You'll fail, old-timer! Your heart isn't in it! But no matter, I'll give you the dignity of knowing you died trying!"

"Put the girl back in the car," Mr. Canis demanded, even over the roaring engine, "or you will experience the kind of bad things I used to do."

The frog-girl laughed. She reached into the backseat with her free arm and grasped for Sabrina, who squirmed and slapped at the disgusting hand but couldn't avoid being yanked out the window by her sweater. The wind slapped her in the face and howled in her ears as she struggled to free herself. Mr. Canis was too far away to do anything, and the frog-girl knew it. If Sabrina and her sister were going to survive, they were going to have to save themselves.

"Daphne! Do you remember Mr. Oberlin?" Sabrina shouted, hoping one of their more abusive foster fathers was still in Daphne's memory.

"From the Bronx?" the little girl asked.

Sabrina nodded.

The expression on Daphne's face told Sabrina her plan wasn't the little girl's favorite. Regardless, Daphne nodded, and together the sisters leaned over and bit the frog-girl hard. The monster shrieked and let go of them. Sabrina grabbed the frame of the window with one hand and her sister with the other, and together they scrambled back into the car.

"What happened?" Granny Relda asked, still pushing hard on the gas.

"It appears I am not the only one in our home with fangs," Mr. Canis said, climbing back into the car.

"Can we get rid of that thing, fast?" Daphne cried. "I need to get home and brush the bleh out of my mouth."

"Don't worry, *lieblings*," Granny said as she made a rough turn onto a gravel road. "I have a plan."

"Relda, are you sure about this?" Mr. Canis asked as he strapped his seat belt around himself.

"Absolutely!"

Sabrina peered through the front windshield and saw a sign blocking the road ahead. It read DANGER! BRIDGE UNSAFE! GO NO FARTHER! Worse was what lay beyond it. In the distance was an old, run-down bridge covering a rocky stream. A mouse couldn't have crossed it safely, let alone an ancient two-ton monstrosity on wheels.

"What's Granny's plan?" Daphne asked, smacking at the frog monster's hand as it snatched at her through the window.

"You don't want to know!" Sabrina replied as she once again strapped Daphne into her seat.

The car crashed through the old wooden sign, and it exploded around them. A giant chunk slid over the roof and, by the sound of the pained groan, smacked the monster in her head. Unfortunately, Granny didn't stop driving, and when the jalopy raced onto the the rickety bridge, Sabrina knew they were in trouble. Creaking beams and snapping wood drowned out the car's backfires and grinding gears. The old bridge tilted to the left just as the car reached the halfway point, and Sabrina saw something that nearly gave her a heart attack. The middle of the bridge was collapsed, leaving a giant hole no car could ever get across.

Granny wasn't slowing down.

"We're not going to make it!" Sabrina shouted, battling the roaring engine to be heard.

"I love pancakes, too!" the old woman shouted back.

I hate this car, Sabrina thought to herself.

"What are you fools doing?" the frog-girl cried.

Granny Relda floored the accelerator, the engine screamed, a flame shot out of the car's muffler, and suddenly they were soaring over the gaping hole. Sabrina looked out the back window and watched their unwanted passenger lose her grip on the car and fly up into the air. When the car landed hard on the other side, the frog-girl did not follow. Sabrina watched the creature crash through the collapsed section of bridge, then watched the structure buckle and collapse into the rocky stream below.

"Woohoo!" Granny cried as she brought the car to a screeching stop. "Oh, boy, did Froggie get the surprise of her life. How exciting was that? Were you excited? I'm having a blast! If you put Relda Grimm behind the wheel, things get done."

Mr. Canis reached over and turned the car off, then pocketed the keys. The car backfired and then sat silently, as if troubled by what had just happened to it. Everyone followed suit, except for Elvis, who whined softly.

"Well, I guess I'll just drive us home now," Granny Relda said.

Everyone shouted "No!" in unison. Sabrina saw the disappointment in her grandmother's face. The old woman slowly got out of the car, and Mr. Canis slid over into the driver's seat. As she got in on the passenger's side, Granny Relda crossed her arms and pouted. It reminded Sabrina of something Daphne would do.

"My driving isn't that bad, is it?" the old woman asked.

"Yes!" everyone shouted.

The family staggered into their home, with Sabrina quietly cursing one of the worst days of her life. They found Puck sprawled across the couch. He had moved several stacks of books away from the television and was watching it with the sound all the way up. Three delivery pizza boxes, countless empty bags of chips, a leaky carton of ice cream, and a half-empty two-liter bottle of soda littered the floor. He balanced a can of spray cheese on his belly, and when he saw the family limp into the house, he lifted the cheese can, sprayed an enormous portion into his mouth, then offered them the can. When no one took him up on his offer, he gargled the greasy orange junk food and swallowed. An enormous, window-rattling belch followed.

"Old lady!" he crowed. "You've been hiding this magic box from me! You can spy on other worlds with it. I just watched a man and his talking car jump across a river!"

Sabrina's exhaustion turn to anger, and from the expressions on the rest of her family's faces, she could see they felt the same way.

While they had been fighting off a frog monster, Puck had been having the best day ever. Life was unfair.

"What?" he asked defensively, spraying more cheese into his mouth.

While Granny cooked dinner, the girls patiently explained to Puck all that had happened at the school and Mayor Charming's house. The boy seemed to think Mr. Grumpner's murder was fascinating and was terribly depressed that he hadn't seen the frog-girl.

"Was she ugly?" he asked.

"Very," Daphne said. "I'm going to have nightmares."

"Why is it that I miss all the fun?" Puck complained.

"I guess you just don't have our luck," Sabrina said.

"Well, I hope the two of you washed your hands when you got home," he said to the girls. "Frogs give you warts, and it sounds like the one you fought off was mighty big. I won't be surprised if you wake up in the morning and find you have turned into giant brown warts."

Daphne's eyes grew as big as saucers. "Uh-uh," she said, though she didn't sound confident.

"It's true. If you hurry and take a bath, it might not be too late!" Puck advised.

The little girl rushed out of the kitchen and could be heard running up to the stairs to the bathroom.

"You shouldn't tease her like that," Sabrina said, vigorously washing her hands at the kitchen sink.

"Puck, do you know the Widow?" Granny Relda asked as she stirred a pot of soup on the stove.

"Of course," Puck replied. "Queen of the crows."

"Could you ask her to come for a visit?" Granny Relda said.

"Why?" he asked. "Are we going to cook her?"

"Of course not," Granny said, horrified. "I have some questions for her. She might be able to help us with our case."

"Since when does the Trickster King act as your messenger, old lady?" the boy asked.

"Since he started living under her roof," Mr. Canis growled. He slammed his fist down hard on the kitchen counter, causing the sugar bowl to lose its lid. "This is serious business, boy. Now go!"

Puck eyed Canis in shock, but after a moment his glistening wings popped out and flapped loudly. He flew quickly through the house and slammed the front door behind him.

Mr. Canis leaned against the table to catch his breath. "I was too hard on him," he said with regret.

Granny Relda patted the old man on his shoulder. "Go and rest."

"There may be more danger," Canis insisted.

"A perfectly good reason to get a little sleep while you can," Granny Relda said. "Go. No arguments."

The old man nodded and shuffled out of the room.

"Who's the Widow?" Sabrina asked.

Granny crossed the room and snatched a large book of fairy tales off a shelf. She placed it in front of Sabrina and smiled. The author was listed as Hans Christian Andersen.

"Hans Christian Andersen wrote about her in 'The Snow Queen.' She's an old friend. She might be able to shed some light on the crow feathers we found. She's sort of an expert on birds. It couldn't hurt for you to read Andersen's account of her."

"Do you think birds had something to do with the murder?" Sabrina asked as she flipped through the heavy book.

"It's hard to say," the old woman said. "But the Widow will know for sure."

Daphne's skin was red from scrubbing and her hair was wrapped up in a big white towel when she and Sabrina gathered in the dining room for dinner. Puck had not returned, and Mr. Canis decided to pass on eating, so the girls took their seats, and Granny served hot soup and buttered rolls to them. Like all of Granny's cooking, the soup took some getting used to. It tasted like warm butterscotch pudding, but Sabrina was so hungry, she didn't have the strength to complain.

Between slurps, the old woman jotted notes in her notebook.

"So let's review what we know. Mr. Grumpner was found dead

inside a giant spiderweb. Black feathers were found at the bottom of a broken window. The Scarlet Hand symbol was left at the scene."

"And we were attacked by Kermit the Frog's evil sister," Daphne added.

"Which is the foundation of my theory. Girls, I believe we have two monsters on our hands now," Granny Relda said.

"Two?" Sabrina cried.

"The frog-girl, for one. But I don't know if she's involved in the murder. That was done by a spider, of course."

"Of course," Sabrina said sarcastically. "Why couldn't it just be the frog-girl?"

"Frogs don't spin webs," Granny said.

"Duh!" Daphne said, then took a big bite of her roll. "A ian ida."

"What?"

Daphne swallowed. "A giant spider," she repeated, then immediately stuffed another oversized bite into her mouth.

"Agreed. One normal-size spider could never trap a human being," Granny Relda said.

"What about Charming's army-of-spiders idea?" Sabrina asked.

"It's still a possibility," Granny said, scribbling more notes in her book.

"If it was an army of spiders, that would explain the broken window," Sabrina said, suddenly realizing how insane the world she now lived in sounded in her ears.

"Maybe," Granny replied.

"You don't think so?" the girl asked.

"The glass was all over the floor, so something certainly came through the window, but the shards were everywhere, which tells us whatever it was came in very fast."

"Urds," Daphne mumbled, with a mouthful of soup.

"Right, birds," Sabrina said. "The black feathers were underneath the window. But that's where I get confused. Were the birds helping the spider monster?"

"Birds and spiders do not work together," Granny Relda explained. "Birds eat spiders."

Granny stood up and crossed the room to a pile of books stacked next to the radiator. She tugged at a couple in the middle of the stack and sent the rest tumbling to the floor. She left the fallen pile where it was and returned to the table.

"This book has just about everything ever written on giant animals," Granny Relda said, setting it in front of the girls. "It's a bit dry, and the author has an unhealthy fear of certain animals, but it might be helpful."

Sabrina eyed the book, entitled *Magical Mutations of Insects, Reptiles, and Kitties.* She opened the cover and saw a crude drawing of a giant kitten chewing on several screaming knights. She flipped to another page, and a thin pamphlet fell out. She picked it up and examined it. The cover read *Rumpelstiltskin's Secret Nature.*

"What's this?" she asked, leafing through it. The pages were filled with tiny, neat writing.

"I've been looking for that for ages!" Granny said. "Your great-aunt Matilda Grimm wrote it."

Daphne took the pamphlet. "Rumpel . . . Rumpel . . . what's this say?"

"It's called *Rumpelstiltskin's Secret Nature*," her grandmother said, taking the booklet from the little girl. "Matilda was obsessed with Rumpelstiltskin. You could say she was a Rumpelstiltskin specialist."

"Isn't that the guy who made the lady guess his real name?" Daphne asked.

Granny nodded. "Matilda had dozens of theories on why he tricked people out of their firstborn children, how he spun gold from straw, where he came from—she thought he could manipulate people into making bad choices. You should read this when you get a chance. Anyone for more camel hump soup?"

Sabrina let the spoonful of soup she was about to put into her mouth drop down into her bowl with a splash. "This is made from a camel's hump?" she cried. Images of a sweaty, flea-covered camel danced around in her mind. She'd seen one at the Bronx Zoo with her father and remembered it spitting at her. She could still smell its rank breath years later. She felt sick.

"Actually, it's two-hump camel soup, but I only use the second hump," Granny Relda explained. "The first hump is a little tough, and besides, it's the second hump that has all the flavor."

The girls stared at the old woman as if she were playing an elaborate joke on them, but Sabrina could see from her expression that she was serious. Of course, Daphne clapped her hands happily and cried, "I'll have more! And this time put some extra hump in there!"

Sabrina slowly pushed her nearly empty bowl away just as she heard a knock on the front door. Granny, who was on her way to the kitchen, stopped and rushed to answer it, with the girls following right on her heels. There on the porch stood a humongous black crow. Its head bobbed nervously, and its squawk was ear-shattering. On one of its legs was a black ribbon, and when it saw the family, it dipped its head in what Sabrina guessed was a bow of respect.

"Good afternoon, Widow," Granny Relda said to the bird.

"Good afternoon to you, Relda Grimm," the crow croaked in a scratchy yet feminine voice.

Daphne squealed in glee and bit down on the palm of her hand, but Sabrina's stomach did a flip-flop. *More talking animals, ugh.*

"Mrs. Grimm, did you know that the little brat you sent plucked a feather out of my behind and laughed?" the crow complained.

"I am deeply sorry," Granny Relda apologized. "I do appreciate you coming for a visit."

"Well, the boy said it was important. I would have come in my human form, but at this time of night the traffic can be killer. I took the Seven down to the Forty and got off at Miller Road, but you know that disaster with all the orange cones, and right now the Eighteen is backed up for miles, so I just parked on the side of the road and transformed. I don't know why I bother with the car. Flying is really the quickest way," the bird croaked.

"Your English is coming along very well," Granny Relda commented.

"Thank you," the crow cawed. "Some of my brothers and sisters refuse to speak anything but Crowish, but I say you have to adapt. It's good to learn new things. I've even taken up paddleboarding."

"What fun!" Granny said with a smile. "I was wondering if you have heard anything about the human who was killed today at the elementary school?"

"Indeed, I have," the Widow replied. "Want to know how I know?"

Granny nodded.

"A little bird told me," the crow said. For a moment, there was silence. "Get it? *A little bird told me?*"

"That's very funny," the old woman said as a pained smile crossed her face. Sabrina rolled her eyes, but Daphne laughed so hard, she snorted.

"Oh, I like the little one." The crow chuckled. "You gotta have a good sense of humor to live in this town."

"That is so true. So, as I was saying, the death was very suspicious, and we found this at the crime scene," Granny Relda said as she took one of the black feathers they had found in the classroom out of her handbag and held it out to the massive bird.

"Yes, it's all the flock can caw about," the Widow said, eyeing the feather.

"Oh?" Granny Relda asked.

The bird hesitated and looked around as if someone might be listening.

"Some of my brothers and sisters can't account for about fifteen minutes of the day," the crow whispered. "They have no memory of what happened. All they know is that they heard music, then *wham!* They were all standing around the schoolyard, unsure of how they got there."

"That is very odd," Granny said. "Have you heard who might be responsible?"

"I think it's fairly obvious, Mrs. Grimm," the crow said. "It was the Scarlet Hand."

"What makes you think so, Widow?" Sabrina asked. Only a few people knew about the red handprint on the blackboard.

"They've sent you a warning, ladies. You're messing around with some very bad people."

"Warning? I don't know what you're talking about," said the old woman.

"You don't know? It's all over your house."

Sabrina, Daphne, and Granny Relda rushed down the porch steps and turned and looked up at the house. On the windows, roof, and even on the chimney were red handprints.

"Who did this?" Sabrina asked.

"How did they do this? We've been home for a while and haven't heard a thing," Daphne added.

The Widow hopped down the steps and flew up into the air. "Keep your nestlings close," the crow squawked, then disappeared over the tree line.

Granny reached down and took the girls by the hand.

"Girls, get back into the house," she said sternly. "We're being watched."

6

I T WAS OBVIOUS TO SABRINA THAT THE SCARLET
Hand had spooked Granny Relda. The old woman spent the
rest of the night silently digging through her old books and
taking notes. When the girls announced they were going to bed,
she barely noticed because she was too busy with her research.

While Daphne brushed her teeth, Sabrina ran her head under
the bathtub faucet and washed her hair for the fourth time that
day, hoping to finally rid her locks of Puck's glue. When they were
both finished, they headed for their bedroom, where they got into
their nightclothes. Daphne pinned her deputy's badge to the front
of her footie pajamas. She brought out its shine with a good buff-
ing, then went to their father's desk, which was slowly morphing
into a beauty parlor, and took a hairbrush from one of its drawers.

"May I?" she asked. Sabrina nodded, and her little sister climbed
up on the bed, took the towel off of the older girl's head, and ran
the brush over her long blond hair. For some reason, brushing

Sabrina's hair helped calm Daphne down so that she could go to sleep. After finding a dead body, being attacked by a frog-girl, nearly dying with Granny behind the wheel of the car, and having the house vandalized right under the Grimms' noses, Daphne would be brushing for a long time, Sabrina suspected.

"You OK?" she asked.

"I can't get Mr. Grumpner's face out of my head," Daphne replied.

"Try not to think about it."

"But we have to think about it. Now that we're police officers, it's up to us to find his killer."

"I think we should let the sheriff handle this one," Sabrina said.

"We made a vow. Besides, we are Grimms, and this is what we—"

"Yes, I know, but is it what we should do? Mom and Dad are still out there, waiting to be found and rescued," Sabrina interrupted.

"We'll find them," her sister promised.

"When? We've been living here for three weeks, and all our time has been spent killing giants, catching Lilliputians, and now tracking giant, murderous spiders. Mom and Dad should be our priority."

"The mayor needs our help."

"Daphne, what if he's just trying to keep us busy so we can't look? How do we know that Charming isn't the one who kidnapped our parents?"

"He wouldn't do that."

"He's an Everafter, Daphne!"

"What is that supposed to mean?" Daphne asked.

"He can't be trusted!" Sabrina exploded.

Daphne looked at her as if she didn't recognize her. It was an expression more hurtful than any word she could have said.

"Daphne, they hate us. Our family locked them in this town. Why wouldn't they want to do us harm? And you saw that handprint as well as I did. Jack wore one on his shirt when he was trying to kill us, and the cops found the same symbol on Dad's abandoned car. It's all connected, and Everafters are behind everything," Sabrina tried to explain.

"Sabrina, not all Everafters are bad."

"How do you know that?" the older girl insisted.

Daphne set the hairbrush on the nightstand, crawled under the covers, and turned her back on her sister.

"I just know," she mumbled.

"Stop being so naive," Sabrina snapped.

"What does *naive* mean?" the little girl asked.

"It means you believe something because you're too dumb to know better," Sabrina said, then immediately regretted how the words came out. She wasn't trying to insult her sister, but the little girl's thinking was so simple and silly.

"I really don't like you very much right now," Daphne said.

Sabrina stared up at the ceiling, feeling too justified to apologize.

Oh, well, it wouldn't be the first time Daphne had given her the silent treatment. She'd get over it.

"You'll see I'm right soon enough," Sabrina said, but there was no response. "Good night."

Her sister said nothing, so Sabrina snatched a copy of *The Blue Fairy Book* off the nightstand and opened it to page one. Maybe there was something in the book, some kind of magic she could use to find their parents. Someone in her family had to do something.

Early the next morning, Sabrina awoke to a thundering racket, followed by a series of thuds and crashes that knocked a picture off the bedroom wall. Something was going on at the end of the hallway that sounded like a fistfight, and Sabrina knew there could be only one source of the chaos—Puck. She eyed the clock, and, since it was only 5:00 a.m., her blood began to boil. Five in the morning was too early for his nonsense.

Of course, Daphne slept through the calamity, snoring away in peaceful slumber. The little girl could doze through World War Three. The only thing she wouldn't sleep through was breakfast.

Sabrina leaped out of bed and marched down the hallway. The terrible prank from the day before had taught her not to barge into the boy's room, so she angrily banged on the door. After several moments, she realized that the tremendous noise wasn't coming from inside Puck's bedroom but from the bathroom down the hall. Fearing her grandmother might have fallen in the tub, Sabrina rushed to the bathroom door, grabbed the knob, and flung it open just as a nearly naked eleven-year-old boy ran past her.

"Puck!" Granny Relda cried. "Come back here!"

Mr. Canis leaped to his feet and rushed past Sabrina, chasing the boy, who fled downstairs.

"What's going on?" Sabrina asked. The bathroom was a complete disaster. The bathtub was surrounded by a dozen empty bottles of shampoo and what looked like the wrappings of at least twenty bars of soap. The inside of the tub was filled with an oily black sludge that slowly spiraled down the drain. On the toilet tank was a bucket where four fat worms, several dead beetles, a hand grenade, and thirty-six cents in change were collected.

"Puck is having his bath . . . his eighth bath," Granny Relda said, partly exhausted and partly annoyed. "You've let him out, and now he's probably in the woods rolling in who knows what . . . again!"

"Not that I'm complaining, but why is he taking a bath?" Sabrina asked suspiciously. Puck hadn't taken a bath since he'd moved into the house, and his unbearable stink had ruined many a meal for her. One whiff of his nauseating aroma was all anyone needed to realize that the Trickster King and soap were bitter enemies.

"We felt it was necessary, under the circumstances," said Granny Relda. Sabrina noticed that the old woman was wearing plastic gloves to protect her hands and a pair of safety goggles.

"Circumstances? What circumstances?"

Before Granny could explain, Mr. Canis stomped into the room with the boy in his arms. Slippery Puck squirmed and kicked the entire way.

"This is rubbish!" he shrieked as the old man wrapped him in a clean towel.

"The tub is clogged again," Granny Relda said. "I suppose we could try another round on the teeth while it drains."

Sabrina eyed the bathroom sink, where four worn-down and abused toothbrushes had met their doom. Several tubes of toothpaste littered the floor, each thoroughly emptied of all its cavity-fighting protection.

"Will someone please tell me what is going on in here?" Sabrina demanded.

Puck turned and smirked at her. A devilish gleam sparkled in his eyes, and he temporarily ceased his indignant protests.

"Guess what, piggy! I'm going to school with you today!" he shouted as he kicked the door closed in her stunned face. "I'm going to be your bodyguard!"

"Yes, you absolutely do need a bodyguard." Granny Relda argued with Sabrina as she tried to pat Daphne's hair down with her hand. The little girl's glue-soaked locks were still forming unusual styles. Today, it looked like a pointy Mohawk that stood about a foot and a half above her head. Sabrina's own hair was super curly after multiple shampoos, producing an almost perfect globe shape, like a big yellow tennis ball. Finding little success with either of them, Granny gave up and turned her attention to serving each girl glow-in-the-dark waffles for breakfast. "We've got a murderer loose in the hallways. I'll feel better if there is someone there to look after you."

"But why Puck?" Sabrina cried. "Why don't you come? You could use a fairy godmother wand to change yourself into a kid."

"I'd look like a kid, but I'd still be an old lady," said Granny. "You need someone a bit more spry than me if something happens."

"Actually," Daphne said, shoveling half a glowing waffle into her mouth, "I think it's a great idea. He looks and acts our age. Plus, he's fun."

Sabrina shot her sister a betrayed look, but the little girl didn't see it. Daphne was still giving Sabrina the cold shoulder. She refused to make eye contact with her older sister and turned back to her breakfast.

"You won't think he's fun when he turns into a monkey and throws his own poop down the hallway," Sabrina said. "And it's not like the kids aren't going to notice him. You can give him all the baths you want, but there are still fifteen layers of crud under his pits. He smells like Coney Island after a clam-eating contest."

"Excuse me?" Puck inquired. The boy had slipped into the room without anyone seeing him. Sabrina turned to give him her usual scowl, but what she saw was shocking. Puck was transformed—clean, shiny, and blond. Every inch of his body was washed, rinsed, and repeated. His previously leaf-infested, raggedy hair had been combed and conditioned, and his teeth sparkled like diamonds. Even his ever-present ratty green hoodie and jeans had been replaced with black cargo pants, a striped baby blue rugby shirt, and brand-new sneakers.

"Puck! You're . . . You're . . ." Sabrina stammered.

"You're a hottie!" Daphne shouted.

Sabrina hated herself, but she agreed. Puck, the shape-shifter, the royal pain-in-the-rear, was . . . cute. She found she couldn't stop staring, even when he caught her.

"Yes, it's true," he said as he took a seat. "I'm beautiful."

Puck grinned at Sabrina, and his big green eyes made her melt.

Granny placed a plate of waffles in front of him, and he shoveled them into his mouth with his bare hands. Whatever spell was cast on Sabrina quickly faded as she watched him pour maple syrup down his throat, then take a greedy bite from a stick of butter.

"Puck!" Granny Relda groaned as she wiped syrup off the boy's face. "Use a fork. You don't want to have to take another bath, do you?"

"Don't worry, old lady," he said with a grin. "I'll behave. Besides, who's going to notice me with these two and their hair?" Suddenly, his head morphed into a donkey's head. He brayed and laughed and spat all over Sabrina.

"Puck, sweetie, no shape-shifting at the table," Granny Relda lectured.

"Just getting it out of my system," the boy said, transforming back to normal. Sabrina wanted to die. Even when he was being disgusting, he was cute.

Puck looked over at Sabrina, who was wiping his spittle off her face. "Hey, ugly, is that your face, or did your neck throw up?"

Sabrina was horrified. Did he think she was ugly? Why would he say such a horrible thing in front of everyone? And then it dawned on her—this beautiful boy sitting across from her was still Puck the Trickster. He was the boy who had dumped her in a tub of goo and put a tarantula in her bed. Puck was still Puck, even after a makeover.

"This is ridiculous," she said. "So you ran the garden hose over him. What about the insanity on the inside?" Sabrina asked. "You're sending him because of all those red handprints we found on the house. For all we all know, he's the one who made them."

"Me?" Puck asked.

"Who else?" she cried. "You're the Trickster King, right? You were pretty mad when Granny sent you to get the Widow. Scaring us to death would be the perfect revenge."

"I think the glue and buttermilk is seeping into your itty-bitty brain," the boy snapped. "I didn't make those handprints. I wasn't even here."

"Why should we believe you?"

"I believe him," Daphne declared. "He always admits when he pulls a prank. He's proud of them."

"Of course I'm proud of them. They're works of art!" the boy crowed.

Sabrina turned to Daphne and fumed. Once again, her own sister had taken Puck's side against her.

"Well, I'm pretty proud of my right hook!" Sabrina shouted, returning her attention to Puck. "Why don't you come over here, and I'll show it to you."

"Lieblings!" Granny shouted. The children spun around to face the old woman. Her face was flushed, and her little button nose was flaring. "Enough with the shouting!"

"He started it!" Sabrina shouted.

"She started it!" shouted Puck.

"And I'm ending it. Puck is going to school with you," Granny Relda said firmly. "It's final."

Everyone sat silently for a moment, staring down at their breakfasts.

"By the way, marshmallow," Puck said to Daphne, breaking the silence, "how many warts did you find this morning?"

The little girl rolled up her sleeves and showed the boy her arms. "Not one!"

Puck sighed. "That's a shame."

"Why?"

"Well, the little ones show up quick and are easy to get rid of, but the big ones, those take a couple days to rise. Those are the kind that grow on the tip of your nose or out of your neck. You have to have surgery to get rid of those."

Daphne shrieked and jumped from her seat. In no time she was running up the steps to the bathroom again.

"You better scrub harder this time!" Puck shouted to the little girl.

"How is Captain Maturity going to keep an eye on both of us at the same time?" Sabrina asked. "Daphne and I aren't in the same grade."

"Puck is there to watch you, Sabrina. Daphne will be safe with Ms. White," Granny replied. "Snow's a good friend. She's volunteered to keep her eye on your sister."

"Don't worry, old lady," Puck crowed. "I'll keep this one out of trouble."

Granny Relda, Mr. Canis, and Puck steered toward Principal Hamelin's office to enroll "His Majesty" in the sixth grade. Sabrina was fairly sure the boy was a moron, so she wondered what Granny planned to do when the principal put Puck in kindergarten.

Sabrina silently escorted her sister to Ms. White's class and watched her enter without so much as a "good-bye," then walked to homeroom alone. She was nearly there when a hand grabbed her from behind and dragged her into the girls' restroom. She spun around, ready to sock her attacker, only to find Bella waiting with a brush and a can of hair spray.

"You need some serious help," she said, ushering Sabrina to the mirror and immediately going to work on her hair. "How did it get this way?"

"It's a long story," Sabrina said sheepishly.

Bella tugged and pulled with her brush, coated Sabrina's head with hair spray, and then tied the unruly mane up with a pink rubber band. Within minutes Sabrina looked more human than she had managed for herself in two days. She was incredibly grateful.

"It'll hold until lunch," Bella said, handing Sabrina the brush and hair spray. "After that, well, we may have to call in a professional."

"Thank you."

"I wish I could say I did it to be nice," Bella said. "You have the seat in front of mine in science class, and with that head of hair, there was no way I was going to be able to see the Smart Board."

Sabrina laughed. It felt good when Bella did the same.

"We'd better get to class," the blond girl said when the bell rang. "Old Battle-Ax will be mad if we're late."

"Didn't you hear?" Sabrina said. "Mr. Grumpner was killed last night."

"I think the fumes from the hair spray are affecting your brain, Sabrina. Who is Mr. Grumpner? Our homeroom teacher is Mrs. Heart."

"Mrs. Heart?"

Bella didn't stick around to explain. She rushed out of the restroom, calling for Sabrina to hurry and follow.

Sabrina hurried to class, prepared for a sea of sad faces. She assumed there would be a ceremony to honor their murdered teacher, maybe some sessions with grief counselors to console them and answer their questions. Everyone would make a giant condolence card and sign it for Mr. Grumpner's wife and family. But when she stepped through the door, the kids acted as if nothing was wrong. Sabrina was shocked. Sure, Mr. Grumpner was a bitter pill to swallow, but he was a human being and had died a horrible death. Didn't anyone care?

Bewildered, Sabrina went to her seat, sat down, and scanned the room for anyone who might need to talk. Perhaps the grief was too great for everyone, and they were putting on brave faces. But, no, not only were there no tears, some kids were actually laughing and goofing off. Across the room, Bella smiled and gave her a thumbs-up.

The world has gone insane! Sabrina thought to herself. *A man died in this classroom less than twenty-four hours ago, and they're acting like it's just another day!*

A roly-poly woman lumbered into the room and set a handful of books down on Grumpner's desk. She wore her flaming-red hair in a bouffant, and her makeup was so thick and garish, it looked as if it has been applied with a paintball gun. Something about her seemed oddly familiar.

"Clam up, losers," she barked. "Yesterday we were talking about transitive verbs. Pass your homework forward and see how badly you did at identifying them."

Sabrina was dumbfounded. Homework?

"Grumpner didn't assign any homework," Sabrina said to the sleepy girl next to her.

"Who?" the girl asked, taking out her assignment and handing it up the aisle.

The teacher glanced around the room, absorbing the faces of her students. When she spotted Sabrina, her mouth twisted into a bitter scowl. It was then that Sabrina recognized her. Sabrina and Daphne had met her when they snuck into the Ferryport Landing Fund-raising Ball. Her new teacher was the Queen of Hearts.

"Grimm," she snapped. "A word, please."

Sabrina reluctantly got up from her desk and joined the woman at the front of the room. She knew from reading *Alice's Adventures in Wonderland* that Mrs. Heart had a short fuse. More than a few citizens of Wonderland were missing their heads because the queen had lost her temper. Now, as she looked into Mrs. Heart's face, it seemed to Sabrina that her own head might be next on the chopping block.

"I know what you are up to, Grimm," the queen said in a low voice.

"I'm not sure what you mean."

"Don't talk to me like I'm a fool. I know you're spying on me," the woman said. "Well, you can tell that old busybody grandmother of yours that she's wasting her time."

"I'm not spying on you," Sabrina said, feeling her anger rise sharply. How dare the woman accuse her of such a thing? The queen didn't even know her.

"I know it drives you Grimms crazy that there are Everafters working around human children."

"I swear, I'm not up to anything. I'm eleven. I have to go to school. It's the law," Sabrina snapped a bit louder than she expected. She looked around the room and noticed that even some of the drowsy kids were listening to their conversation. She flushed with embarrassment. Mrs. Heart clearly brought out the worst in her.

"I'm watching you, child. Step out of line just once with me, and it's . . ."

"It's what? Off with my head?" Sabrina was shouting, but she couldn't seem to stop herself. Every nerve was aflame with anger and frustration. Her head was pounding, and she felt hot with a fever. "You're a paranoid old kook. If you want to start off like this on your first day, be my guest!"

"First day?" the queen said nervously. "Sabrina, I've been teaching this class since the beginning of the year. Don't you remember?"

Sabrina scanned the classroom as a wave of understanding overtook her. The reason no one was upset about Grumpner's murder, why no one even remembered him, was because their memories had been erased. Charming and his witches must have covered the entire town in forgetful dust. The only reason Sabrina remembered was because her house was protected by magic. She didn't know why she was so surprised. The lousy Everafters were always making inconvenient things disappear. When something got in the way, it vanished, swept under the rug with the flick of a magic wand or a witch's spell. They'd done the same to her parents. They'd do it to the rest of her family if they got the chance.

Sabrina turned back to Mrs. Heart and pointed a finger at the horrible woman's face. "You tell your dirty Everafter friends that they can't erase everything. I'm going to find my mom and dad. And I'm going to find who killed Mr. Grumpner, too!"

Mrs. Heart reeled in shock. Sabrina knew she had betrayed an unspoken rule of Ferryport Landing—never out an Everafter— but she was tired of secrets. Mrs. Heart and the rest of her kind couldn't get away with killing a person and then hiding it.

Suddenly, Wendell rushed into the room. He looked confused

for a moment as he spotted the queen, but he quickly recovered and hurried down the aisle to his seat. The same odd, chalky dust Sabrina kept seeing trailed behind him like a faint cloud. The boy sat down awkwardly and hid his face in his textbook.

"Take your seat, Ms. Grimm," the queen said between gritted teeth. The angry girl marched back to her desk. She spotted Toby, the bug-eyed boy, laughing at her the whole way.

"Mrs. Heart, I'm sorry to interrupt," a voice said from the doorway. Principal Hamelin stepped inside with Puck. "I'd like to introduce a new student. Class, this is Robin Goodfellow."

"Ta-da," Puck sang, waving and bowing as if he were a movie star. "Please, don't make a fuss."

"Robin moved here from . . . um . . . Akron, Ohio, and he'll be staying with Sabrina Grimm's family," Hamelin announced.

"Robin Goodfellow?" the queen muttered knowingly. It was obvious to Sabrina that the teacher recognized the boy.

Puck winked at her. "That's my name—don't wear it out," he crowed.

"Take a seat in the back. There's one near your friend."

The boy looked around the room. "Is that the only seat available? The Grimm girl has a very foul odor," he said with a wicked grin. "She's a real stinker."

The half of the class that wasn't asleep roared with laughter, and Sabrina blushed.

"And she's got quite a temper, too," the queen replied. "Sorry, Mr. Goodfellow. If the rest of the class has to suffer, so do you."

The students roared again.

"So, Mrs. Heart, he's all yours," the principal said, and he left the room.

Sabrina's head was still pounding, and she felt feverish. The anger came so quickly. She glanced around the room and noticed that kids were staring at her. The only students who didn't seem to care were sound asleep. Sabrina lowered her head and took deep breaths to calm down.

"Ms. Grimm," Mrs. Heart said as she marched down the aisle. She stood over Sabrina with her grade book in hand. "No homework today?"

Sabrina's efforts to calm down flew out the window. Her eyes flared as they met the queen's. "I didn't know we had any homework today," she snapped. "But you already know that."

"That's unfortunate, Ms. Grimm," the teacher said with a wicked smile. "I'm going to have to give you a zero. Since you're having trouble keeping up with your assignments, maybe we should set up some special time for you to get them done. I'll see you in detention after school."

"What's detention?" Puck asked.

"It means I have to stay after school for an hour," Sabrina whispered.

"An hour!" The boy laughed. "She can force you to stay here longer than you have to? That's twisted and depraved punishment. I've only been here for five minutes, and it's already an intolerable agony!"

"Mr. Goodfellow, you will join her," Mrs. Heart said.

"Your Majesty!" Puck cried, leaping from his seat. He threw his arms around the woman and wailed. "Show some mercy!"

The Queen of Hearts waited patiently for Puck's dramatics to end and for the students to stop giggling. When he released her, the teacher spun around and headed to the front of the classroom.

"Now, class, let's talk about past participles," she said, turning toward the chalkboard. On the queen's back was a sheet of paper that read I KISS GOATS. The kids who were awake fell over themselves laughing.

The teacher spun around and flashed the class a mascara-heavy evil eye. She turned back to the board, and the class exploded again.

"Anyone who wants to join Ms. Grimm and Mr. Goodfellow in detention, just keep it up!" she shouted.

Sabrina glanced over to Wendell. The odd boy was busy, unfolding a map of the town and writing on it with an ink pen. He was completely oblivious to the events unfolding in the class, and she realized he hadn't even noticed when his own father came into the room. There was something else unusual about him, as well. His feet were covered in white chalk, just like the dust she had found in the halls the night before, after discovering Mr. Grumpner's body. It suddenly dawned on her that those footprints might belong to him.

By the time the bell rang, the entire class was looking at Puck as if he were a rock star.

"Hilarious!" one kid snorted as the students emptied into the hall. Puck absorbed their praise like a greedy sponge and agreed with each one wholeheartedly. According to Puck, he was indeed a genius. Sabrina had no interest in Puck's groupies. Her eyes were glued to Wendell. She watched him hurry down the hallway, leaving a cloud of dust behind him. She rushed to follow.

"Hey, stinkpot," Puck said, breaking away from his fans. "You're not supposed to leave my sight."

Sabrina didn't reply. Instead, she darted through crowds and dodged around open lockers as she trailed the chubby boy. He raced down a flight of stairs and slipped through a door, but by the time Sabrina caught up to him, he had slammed the door behind him. A sign on it read BOILER ROOM.

"Where are you going?" Puck asked, grabbing Sabrina's wrist and pulling her back before she could open the door.

"That Wendell kid knows something about Grumpner's death," she replied, reaching for the door. "I'm going to follow him, if you let go of me."

"You're not supposed to run off without me."

"Well, you're here now. Let's go."

"Sorry, but we're on a tight schedule. I have toilets to clog and overflow. You know, making chaos doesn't just happen. It's a lot of hard work."

"Puck, he went into the boiler room. I bet it's dirty and gross in there," Sabrina said, trying to play to the boy's biggest weakness—filth. "I bet there's a greasy floor you could roll around on and ruin your shirt."

Puck's eyes lit up, and he nodded vigorously. It was nice to see that she could manipulate him when it was important. She reached for the doorknob again, but before she could turn it, a muscular, grizzled-looking man stepped in her way.

"Where do you kids think you're going?" he asked. He was tall and strong, with arms as big as tree trunks and a chest as wide as the family car. The patch on his blue coverall uniform told them his name was Charlie, and the smell coming off of him told them his uniform needed a trip to the Laundromat. But it was the mop slung over his shoulder that told them this was the school janitor, and the boiler room was his domain.

"I was looking for my next class," Sabrina lied.

"In the boiler room?" Charlie laughed, spraying his corned-beef-and-cigarette breath all over her. "Ain't nothing in there but a bunch of toilet brushes and brooms."

"Toilet brushes!" Puck squealed happily. "That sounds disgusting. Can I have one?"

Charlie gave the kids a confused look.

"Our mistake," she said. Together she and Puck headed down the hallway. She snuck a peek back, hoping Charlie had moved on, but he was still there, leaning against the door.

"I could lure him upstairs and push him out a window," Puck offered.

"No, you can't do that. We'll come back later. For now, just go to your next class," Sabrina replied. "Where is it?"

She snatched his schedule out of his hand and looked at it. "Puck, you're in all my classes!"

"The old lady and Canis negotiated it with the principal," the boy explained.

Sabrina knew what kind of negotiating Mr. Canis could do. Now Sabrina would have Puck practically riding on her back.

There were several kids walking behind them, and one of them laughed loudly and said, "Hello, Smelly Stinkpot."

Sabrina spun around to see who had insulted her, but the kids had just walked away.

"Smelly Stinkpot? How dare he?" Sabrina asked Puck.

"Who knows?" he said. "Kids can be cruel."

It would be hours before Bella stopped her in the hallway and removed a sign Puck had taped onto Sabrina's back. It read, PLEASED TO MEET YOU. I'M SMELLY STINKPOT.

The rest of the day, Sabrina and Puck kept a watchful eye out for Wendell, but he appeared to have vanished. During a break between classes, Puck even rushed outside and summoned some pixies with his flute to look for their chubby suspect.

As Sabrina and Puck waited to hear more, they went from one class to the next, and in each the Trickster King did his best to humiliate his housemate. Unlike a normal kid, Puck didn't bring pencils or a notebook to class; he brought what he called the essentials: a squirt gun, stink pellets, a shock buzzer, and his personal favorite—a whoopee cushion.

Now, to Sabrina, fart jokes were old-fashioned. She believed kids were pretty sophisticated in the twenty-first century and that it would take more than an obnoxious noise to get a modern kid laughing. Unfortunately, she was wrong. Puck let the whoopee cushion go in every class, making it seem as if Sabrina were having intestinal issues, and the kids thought it got funnier and funnier. Eventually, he added a little acting to his routine, pretending to gag on Sabrina's imaginary fumes. When this proved to be wildly popular, as well, it quickly evolved into an elaborate death scene, which ended with Puck shaking in convulsions on the floor. His performances, and Sabrina's threats of a serious beating, helped the two rack up an impressive five detentions apiece by midday. At the rate they were going, Sabrina suspected they would be in detention until she was twenty-five.

So as they headed for gym class, she smiled, knowing revenge was within her grasp. Puck was about to get what he had coming to him.

"OK, class," Ms. Spangler said as she tossed a ball back and forth between her hands. "We've got a new student today. His name is Robin, and he says he's never actually played dodgeball."

Even from across the room, Sabrina could see Toby's and Natalie's eyes light up with excitement. Bella, who was standing nearby, leaned over to her. "Your friend is in serious trouble. You should warn him."

Sabrina grinned. "He'll be fine."

Puck waved to everyone, unaware that attention was the last thing he wanted in this class. Once the class got an eyeful of him, Ms. Spangler divided them into two teams. Puck and Sabrina found themselves standing next to each other.

"How do you play this game?" he asked.

"People throw balls at you," she said. "If they hit you, then you're out."

"Let me get this straight. The object of this game is to hit someone with a ball. Can you hit them in the head?"

Sabrina nodded, watching the opposing team to avoid a sneak attack.

"And you can hit them as hard as you want?"

"That's actually encouraged. But be careful—if they catch your throw, you're out."

"Does anyone ever catch the ball?"

"Rarely."

Puck rubbed his hands together eagerly. "It's so twisted, it's brilliant! Are you any good at this 'dodgeball'?"

"I used to be," Sabrina grumbled.

Toby and the big goon, Natalie, were on the opposing team, and both of them were staring at her with evil grins. They were like vultures, waiting to take a bite out of her.

Ms. Spangler blew her whistle, and a ball whizzed past Sabrina's head and smacked right into Bella. Sabrina was surprised. The day before, the girl had been so agile, but now it seemed like Bella had actually stepped into the ball, as if she wanted to be knocked out of the game.

The blond girl shrugged her shoulders. "Good luck," she said to Sabrina as she made her way over to the sidelines.

Toby winged his ball straight at Sabrina's head, and just before it smashed her in the nose, Puck reached over and caught it.

"Toby's out!" Ms. Spangler shouted. Dejected, the boy scowled and sulked over to the sidelines.

"Now what do I do with it?" Puck asked.

"Throw it at somebody," Sabrina said impatiently.

Puck wound up, ready to smack Sabrina right in the face with the ball.

"Not me, you idiot!" she cried, pointing at the other team. "Them!"

Puck threw his ball at a red-haired boy standing close to the front. It rocketed across the room like a missile, hit the redheaded kid in the chest, and sent him flying backward ten yards. The class stopped playing and let out a collective gasp.

"Kevin is out!" Ms. Spangler said, unsympathetic to the boy's obvious injuries.

Every kid looked at Puck as if he had just suggested adding another day to the school week. Puck was public enemy number one. Balls came from every direction, and the boy managed to duck, jump, and somersault around every one. He bent in impossible directions that no normal human being ever could. He stood on his hands and let balls fly between his feet. He taunted everyone, which only made them want to smash him in the face even more. Puck, however, began to collect their weak tosses. In no time he had collected almost every ball in the game and laid them at his feet. When the kids realized his strategy, they whimpered. Even Natalie let out a little cry.

Puck picked up the first of his collection and winged it at a boy standing nearby. The ball hit the kid so hard, he slid across the floor and out the gym doors. Puck picked up another ball, and another, and another, tossing them at impossible speeds. A tall, skinny girl was hit so hard, her shoes flew off her feet. One ball hit a group of kids, bouncing off of one and then hitting the next and the next, until they all tipped over like bowling pins. Even Ms.

Spangler got cracked hard in the back and nearly swallowed her whistle. By the time it was over, Sabrina, Puck, and Natalie were the only ones left standing.

"No boundaries!" Ms. Spangler said.

"What's that mean?" Puck asked.

"It means we can go after her," Sabrina said, pointing at Natalie.

He clapped his hands like a happy baby. "School is awesome!" he shouted. He picked up a ball and handed it to Sabrina.

Sabrina was so happy, she could have kissed Puck. Quickly shaking off this thought, she helped him stalk the big girl around the gym. Natalie huffed like an angry bull.

"You'll drop those balls right now if you know what's good for you," she threatened them.

"You're probably right," Sabrina said, throwing a ball at the girl as hard as she could. It smashed into the side of Natalie's face, and she fell down. It was the second time in two days that Sabrina had knocked the girl off her feet.

"Natalie is out!" Ms. Spangler shouted. "No sides!"

Sabrina turned to congratulate Puck, just as a ball crashed into the side of her face and sent her reeling. The class cheered, and Puck raised his hands in triumph.

"I won!" he cried, then ran around the gym shouting, "Victory lap!"

ᘒ

By the time lunch rolled around, Sabrina was ready to strangle the boy. So when she saw Daphne's smiling face in the cafeteria, it was like seeing a rainbow. The little girl was surrounded by her classmates, who, as they had the day before, hovered around her. When Daphne spotted Sabrina and Puck, she excused herself and joined them at a table in the far corner of the room.

"How has your day been?" she asked.

"It's been horrible," Sabrina said.

"Tell my sister I wasn't talking to her," Daphne said to Puck. "I was talking to you."

Puck grinned. "The squirt says she isn't talking to you."

Sabrina rolled her eyes. "How long are you going to be mad at me?"

"Remind my sister that I just said I was not talking to her," the little girl said to Puck.

"Get over it!" Sabrina cried.

"Tell my sister that when she stops being a snot, I will get over it."

"She says when you stop being a disgusting, booger-crusted freak, she will honor you with a conversation, but until then, shove off," Puck said.

"This is ridiculous," Sabrina huffed, staring down at her serving of not-so-green green beans.

"Ask my sister what *ridiculous* means," Daphne said.

"She wants to know what—"

"I heard her!" Sabrina growled at the boy. "It means you are being silly! It means you are being a baby!"

"Tell my sister that I'm rubber and she's glue, and whatever she says bounces off me and sticks to her."

"Your sister says—"

"Puck!" Sabrina shouted. She turned back to her food and took a bite of something she guessed was chicken. She guessed wrong.

"Well, Daphne, if you don't want to talk to me, then you don't want to know that I've found a clue," she said.

Daphne's face lit up as bright as the sun. "What kind of clue?"

"Are you done with the silent treatment?" her sister asked.

"It depends on how good the clue is."

"You know those dusty footprints we were following last night? Well, there's a kid in my homeroom whose feet were covered in the same dust. I tried to follow him, but he slipped into the boiler room," Sabrina said. "We're going to have to come back after everyone's gone and do some snooping."

Daphne smiled and hugged Sabrina. "Very clever," the little girl said. "I'll talk to you again."

Puck sniffed the creamed corn on his tray. He reached down with his bare hand and scooped some up. Then he licked it with his tongue. "Any of those disgusting warts show up yet?"

"Ms. White told me that you don't get warts from touching frogs," the little girl growled. "Not even frog-girls."

"Ah, I'm sorry to see that little joke die." The boy sighed as creamed corn dripped down his wrist and onto his clean shirt. "I had you completely freaked out."

"Hardy-har-har, Puck. You are so un-punk rock," Daphne said, turning her attention to her sister. "So what's the plan?"

"First, you have to get a detention," Sabrina said as she eyed her gray hamburger.

"What?" Daphne cried.

"Puck got us in trouble, so we have to stay after school. Since the two of us have to stay, you might as well get in trouble, too. We should try to stick together."

"How am I supposed to get a detention?" the little girl asked.

"I don't know! Insult your teacher or something."

"I can't do that to Ms. White!"

"Yes, you can. Be annoying!" Sabrina suggested. "You do it to me every day."

Daphne looked as if she was going to cry.

When the children met at the end of the last period, Daphne was back to giving Sabrina the silent treatment. She wouldn't explain how she got her detention, nor would she look Sabrina in the eye. Sabrina shrugged. If she worried every time her sister got mad at her, she'd never have time to do anything else. Daphne would get over it. The important thing was that they were all together. Nothing bad could happen when they were together.

They walked down the hallway toward the detention room. Puck had nothing but complaints.

"I can't believe I have to be subjected to this torture," he whined. "I am royalty. To say anything I do is inappropriate is nothing short of criminal. Everything I do is majestic and regal."

"So when you were picking your nose in Mr. Cafferty's class, that was regal?" Sabrina asked.

"Absolutely," he said. "Back home people stand out in the freezing rain for days just to hear a rumor that I picked my nose."

"Ugh."

"This detention is going to be horrible. I've heard stories. Some kids go in and never come out, and the ones who do are never the same."

"Aren't you being a little dramatic?"

"Not at all!" Puck insisted. "Whatever that means."

Sabrina rolled her eyes and opened the detention room door. Immediately she put her hand over Daphne's eyes. Mrs. Heart lay on her back in one corner of the room. Snow White was struggling to her feet in another, and in the center was a skeleton in shredded coveralls with a name patch still visible—CHARLIE. The mark of the Scarlet Hand was on the skeleton's chest.

"See, I told you!" Puck said proudly.

"Daphne, don't look," Sabrina said.

Daphne pulled herself away from her sister and rushed to Ms. White. The teacher didn't look seriously injured, but she seemed dizzy and disoriented. The children helped her to her feet and sat her at one of the desks in the classroom. When Ms. White was settled, Sabrina kneeled down to check on Mrs. Heart. She was breathing normally, but she was out cold.

"What happened?" Sabrina asked.

Ms. White looked confused and mumbled, but only one word was distinguishable: "Wendell."

"Wendell did this?" Daphne asked.

Suddenly, there was a loud thump outside, followed by a pained moan. The children ran to the window, and there was Wendell, lying flat on his back on the ground below. The boy had obviously jumped out the window. When he saw the children looking at him, Wendell climbed to his feet and darted off toward the woods as fast as his chubby legs could carry him.

"Hey!" Sabrina shouted. "Come back here!"

Puck's enormous wings burst out of his back. "I'll get him."

Sabrina grabbed his arm before he could fly away. "No. Someone might see you!" she cried, dragging Puck back from the window. Instead, she crawled out herself, dropping five feet before landing safely on the ground. Daphne followed, and then Puck, whose wings had vanished into his back.

"He's headed for the forest!" Puck shouted, and the three children sprinted across the field in hot pursuit. Wendell was not a fast runner, but his big head start allowed him to disappear into the forest long before the children even reached the tree line.

"We lost him," Sabrina groaned.

"No, he left a trail," Puck said, pointing at deep, muddy footprints, and he led the others into the forest. They followed the footprints up a hill, then along a creek, dodging rocks and slippery slopes.

"He's confused," Puck continued. "He goes in one direction and then turns back and runs the other way."

"Why?" Sabrina asked.

"Because he's a moron?" Puck said. "It's slowing him down. We'll find him soon."

The children continued their search, weaving in and out of the thick brambles and leaping over downed trees. Soon, Puck was proven correct. They cornered Wendell against a steep, rocky wall. When he realized he couldn't escape, Wendell whimpered like a dog.

"There's nowhere to go," Puck said. "We know you're the killer. We'll take you back and call the cops. It'll all be over in no time. Don't worry, I hear the electric chair only hurts for a second."

"It's not what you think," Wendell begged, wiping his nose with his handkerchief. "I didn't hurt anyone."

"Then why are you running?" Sabrina asked.

"I'm trying to help!" he cried. "I'm trying to stop them."

"Stop who?" Daphne asked.

"The less you dames know, the better off you'll be," Wendell said, his voice taking on an odd accent, like he was a character in one of the old movies Sabrina's mother loved to watch on weekends, the kind that were in black and white and featured tough-guy detectives.

"Dames?" Sabrina and Daphne exclaimed.

"This is for your own good, sweethearts," Wendell said as he pulled a small harmonica out of his pants pocket and raised it to his lips. He blew a long, high note, and the whole forest erupted with chatter and scurrying. The noises grew louder and louder, and Sabrina wondered if at any moment some horrible monster or giant was going to charge out of the brush. But the noise suddenly stopped, and a furry brown bunny hopped out from behind a tree. It was the cutest thing she had ever seen as it bounded over to them and stopped at their feet. It looked up at the children with soft, warm eyes and made a little twittering noise.

"Oh, look at you!" Daphne cried as she knelt down to pet it. "You are adorable!"

The rabbit snapped viciously at her finger and let out a horrible, angry hiss.

"Evil bunny!" the little girl said, yanking her hand away.

"So that's what your harmonica does?" Puck laughed. "It sends a rabbit to kill us?"

Wendell didn't say anything. He didn't have to. His silence was filled by the sound of hundreds of rabbits pouring into the clearing. They jostled with one another for room, then turned and faced Wendell as if he were some kind of general.

"Guys, I forgot to tell you the other clue I discovered," Sabrina said nervously. "Wendell is the son of an Everafter. The Pied Piper is his father, the same guy who controlled all those rats. I guess magic runs in the family."

Puck laughed. "Wendell, if you think a bunch of hairy little garden thieves are going to stop us, you are sadly mistaken. Call off your furballs, or I'm going to skin the lot of them and make the warmest winter coat you've ever seen!"

Wendell lifted his harmonica to his mouth, and another note sang through the air. The rabbits instantly turned and faced the kids. Their soft brown eyes were now red with anger, their muscles twitched eagerly, and their mouths opened wide.

"Get them!" Wendell shouted, and the first wave of the furry zombie army sprang at the children.

7

T HAT'S THE BEST YOU CAN DO?" PUCK SHOUTED, spinning on his heels and transforming into a massive thirteen-foot brown bear. He roared so viciously that Sabrina felt it in her toes, but it didn't intimidate the rabbits. They dove onto him in waves, knocking his mammoth body to the ground and covering him from head to toe.

"Puck!" the girls shouted, terrified that he'd been killed. And for a brief moment it seemed as if their fears were true. But the boy soared out of the bunny pile and into the sky, giant wings flapping. He dipped back down, snatched each girl by the hand, and began an awkward effort to fly out of the forest.

"Next time, why don't one of you tell me to shut up?" Puck cried.

"As if you'd listen," Sabrina snarled.

"I am so going to have nightmares about this," Daphne sobbed. "Bunnies are ruined for me forever!"

Puck sailed through the woods, barely managing to avoid the

giant cedars and fir trees that seemed to appear out of nowhere. He ducked between branches and flapped fiercely to soar over the brush and pricker bushes on the forest floor. One desperate effort to dodge a huge maple tree forced him to dive close to the ground, where one of the rabbits leaped up and sank its teeth into Sabrina's pant leg. She shook it off, and it disappeared into the furry sea below.

"Head for the river!" Sabrina cried. "They can't follow us over the water."

Puck frowned at her. "I know what I'm doing," he growled.

"If you knew what you were doing, we wouldn't have two million zombie bunnies chasing us!" she shouted.

"Guys," Daphne said, trying to get their attention.

"How was I supposed to know that kid was mentally unhinged?" Puck asked.

"I don't know," Sabrina barked. "Maybe when we found him running from a skeleton?"

"Guys!" Daphne shouted.

"What?" Puck and Sabrina snapped.

"LOOK OUT!"

Sabrina looked up to see a two-story-high fence in front of them. Puck made a desperate swerve and narrowly missed smashing into it, then dove right back into the argument.

"I don't know why I'm involved in this, anyway!" he cried. "I'm one of the bad guys!"

"The only bad thing about you is your breath!" Sabrina shouted. "All we ever hear about is Puck the villain! What kind of villain has creamed corn all over his shirt?"

"You want to see how bad I can be?" he growled. "I'll show you!"

Puck soared into the backyard of someone's home, where they saw a stocky senior citizen puttering around. As the trio flew above the man, they heard him shout, "Agnes! The rabbits have been digging up the yard again. I swear, the next one I see is going to wish it had never been born!"

Puck howled with laughter as he led the bunnies right through the poor man's yard. By the time the old fellow saw them coming, it was too late. The bunnies stampeded over him. Sabrina caught a glimpse of his shocked face as the bunnies knocked him to the ground.

"That was mean!" Daphne shouted at Puck.

"You ain't seen nothin' yet," the boy crowed.

Flapping vigorously, the boy flew across the street just as an old woman's car came to a stop at the intersection. She was a tiny old lady who could barely see over her dashboard. She must have been legally blind, too, because she waited patiently, unblinking, for Puck and the two girls to fly across the road, followed by a couple thousand rabbits. When her way was clear, she drove off as if nothing unusual had happened at all.

"People are going to see us! You've got to get us off the street," Sabrina insisted.

"Your wish is my command," Puck yelled. He flew straight toward a house as a tall man opened his front door. When he bent over to pick up his newspaper, Puck flew through the open doorway, dragging the girls along.

"No! Don't!" Daphne cried as Puck sailed through the living room with the wave of rabbits tumbling through the house behind them. Puck flew into the dining room, where two small children were setting the table, oblivious to what was headed in their direction. They were too busy hungrily eyeing a glistening golden ham at the center of a dinner feast. Daphne accidentally kicked the ham and a bowl of mashed potatoes onto the floor. Two hyperactive English springer spaniels raced into the room and tore into the fallen food.

"Chelsea! Maxine! No!" the mother shouted, running in from the kitchen and desperately trying to drag the remains of the ham from their greedy mouths. "Bad dogs!"

A moment later, the entire family was drowning in bunnies.

Puck flew into the kitchen, then blasted through the back door and zipped outside. The rabbits crashed through windows and knocked the back door off its hinges, gaining ground with every second.

Sabrina looked up at Puck and saw the smug grin on his face.

"Proud of yourself?" she snapped.

"Yes," he said.

"They're still coming!" Daphne cried. "We have to go somewhere they can't."

"We're on our way," Puck said. Soon they were out of the neighborhoods and flying back over acres of overgrown woods. In no time, the Hudson River stretched out before them. A tiny island sat in the middle, with the ruins of what looked like a dilapidated castle.

"If we fly out over the river, they won't be able to follow," Sabrina said.

"Oh, we're going over the river all right, but not to save you from the rabbits!" Puck cried. "We're going over because you questioned my villainy."

Sabrina looked up into his face. "You wouldn't dare!"

"That's another thing you shouldn't question!"

He flapped his wings hard, and soon the three were soaring over the rocky cliffs, high above the churning Hudson. Sabrina watched the rabbits race to the cliff's edge and then abruptly stop.

"I hope you two brought some towels," Puck said.

"Don't do it!" Sabrina demanded.

But before Puck could dump them into the icy water, his body buckled as if he had flown into a brick wall. Sabrina lost her grip on him and dropped like a stone, landing hard in the freezing river below. She sank deep into the water, then swam frantically to reach the surface in time to see Daphne splash down beside her.

"Daphne!" she screamed. She dove into the water, and, after several moments of frenzied searching, her already numb fingers found something soft. It was Daphne! Sabrina wrapped her arms around her sister and pulled her to the surface.

The little girl gasped for air and started choking as a mouthful of water spilled from her lips.

"Where's Puck?" she asked between painful coughs.

Sabrina scanned the waves nearby, but there was no sign of the boy.

"Puck!" she shouted, but there was no response. The girls took turns calling for him.

"You need to get to shore. Can you swim there on your own?" Sabrina asked.

Daphne nodded, but her face was panicked.

"He's tough," Sabrina reminded her. "Just get to shore. I'll keep looking." She let her sister go, and the little girl doggy-paddled toward land. Luckily, their father had taught them both how to swim at the YMCA near their old apartment. Daphne was like a fish. She'd be fine.

"Puck!" Sabrina shouted again, and when he didn't respond, she took a deep breath and dove back into the cold water. She swam in circles, back and forth, searching in the murky waves with her hands but finding nothing. Finally, her lungs ached for oxygen, and she was forced to return to the surface.

Gasping for breath, she noticed something odd floating in the distance. When she looked closer, she knew what it was—a striped blue rugby shirt. She swam as hard as she could and found Puck facedown in the water. She turned him over. His face was blue. She had to get him to shore. She wrapped one arm around his cold body and swam as best she could. Once she reached the shore, Daphne helped her drag the motionless boy onto dry ground.

"Please don't be dead, Puck!" the little girl cried.

"Stand back," Sabrina said. "I'm going to try CPR."

She tilted the boy's head and looked in his mouth for obstructions, remembering the lifesaving lessons they'd taught her in school. Her only experience was on a rubber dummy—never on a real, live person! She tried not to think about the C-minus she got for the course.

Sabrina took a deep breath and placed her mouth on Puck's, blowing all her air down his windpipe. Nothing happened. She did it again, then remembered she needed to press on his sternum to force air in and out of his lungs. She counted off fifteen compressions with the palms of her hands, then returned to blowing into his mouth.

Suddenly, his eyes opened, and he shoved Sabrina away.

"Ack! I'm contaminated!" he cried, wiping his mouth.

"Puck, you're alive!" Daphne shouted and hugged the boy.

"Of course I'm alive," the boy said, crawling to his feet. "A dip in the river can't kill the Trickster King."

"We thought . . . you were . . . I tried . . ." Sabrina stammered.

"You thought you'd give me a kiss while I was napping," Puck said indignantly. "I'm going to have to stop taking baths if you can't keep your hands to yourself."

Sabrina was so angry, she was sure steam was coming out of her ears.

"What happened?" Daphne asked.

"We slammed into the barrier. The one that keeps Everafters from leaving Ferryport Landing. Magic is pretty hard." Puck laughed.

"You think this is funny?" Sabrina snapped. "We could have died out there."

"Now who's being dramatic?" he said.

"Children?" a soft voice called out from behind them. They spun around and found Ms. White standing on the banks of the river. "We need to get you out of this cold."

"Well, I knew something was strange. I never had a student ask me for a detention before," the pretty teacher said, winking at Daphne, who sat in the front seat of the car with her. Puck and Sabrina shivered in the backseat under blankets.

"Knowing your father as I did, I figured the two of you were up to something, so I thought I'd better come down to the detention room and find out for sure. When I got there, the Queen of Hearts was trying to fight off the monster with a chair," she continued.

"Was it a giant spider or a frog-girl?" Sabrina asked.

"Neither!" Snow White replied. "This was more like a wolf or a gorilla or, well, both."

"Another monster?" Daphne said.

"This town is lousy with them," Puck said.

"I think it ate Charlie. It was going after the queen next, but, lucky for her, I arrived. I fought it, but it was so strong."

"What did you do?" asked Daphne.

"Nothing. I didn't have to. Wendell saved us," the teacher continued. "He blew into his harmonica, and the music seemed to stop the monster, at least for a second, before it jumped out the window and ran off. Wendell was chasing after it when you saw him. I tried to tell you, but you didn't listen."

"How do you know he was trying to save you? Maybe he was trying to help that thing escape," Sabrina said.

"Oh, no!" Snow White argued. "That sweet little boy had nothing to do with this."

"Ms. White, when we confronted him, he sent an army of rabbits after us," Sabrina said. "Besides, you can't put anything past an Everafter."

"Sabrina!" Daphne cried.

"What's that supposed to mean?" the teacher asked.

"No offense," Sabrina replied. "But everything about your kind is deceptive. You hide behind magic, and when something bad happens, you make it disappear. Poof! None of the kids at school remember Mr. Grumpner. Tomorrow they won't remember Charlie. Then there's the fact that most Everafters wish my family was dead."

"I'm not hiding, young lady," Ms. White replied coolly as she pulled her car into Granny's driveway. "And I don't wish your family was dead. Not all Everafters are alike."

Before Sabrina could argue, Granny Relda and Elvis came running out to meet them.

"*Lieblings*, where have you been?" their grandmother asked, rushing down the driveway as the children climbed out of the car. Elvis was so excited to see Daphne, he accidentally knocked her down with a series of excited kisses.

"In the river," the little girl said. "It was fun but very cold."

"In the river?" Granny Relda asked. "Why were you in the river?"

"The rabbits chased us there," Daphne replied matter-of-factly.

The old woman threw her hands into the air. "What are you talking about?"

"I found them near Bannerman's Island. They've had quite an

afternoon, Relda," Ms. White said as she got out of her car. "They could use some warm clothes and some soup."

"Thank you for bringing them home, Snow," the old woman said, taking the teacher's hand.

"My pleasure," Snow White said. She turned and went back to her car, but then, suddenly, she turned and eyed Sabrina. "I hope you'll think about what I said. You can't judge the many by the actions of the few."

Granny raised a curious eyebrow at Sabrina as the teacher drove away but didn't press her granddaughter for an explanation.

"*Lieblings*, we have to get you into the bath," the old woman said. "Daphne, you go first, and make that water good and warm."

Daphne nodded, shot Sabrina an angry look, and rushed into the house with Elvis at her heels.

"I think I'll go up to my room," Puck said.

"Absolutely not!" Granny Relda commanded. "You're next in the bathtub."

The boy's face tightened as if he had just bitten into a lemon. "I have a reputation, you know. What will people say if they hear an old lady is forcing me to use soap and water every ten minutes?" he demanded. "I'll be the laughingstock of every tree gnome, pixie, hobgoblin, and brownie from here to Wonderland."

"Everyone is just going to have to think a little less of you, then," Granny said. "Now, rush upstairs and change out of those clothes."

Puck pouted, but Granny Relda didn't budge. After several moments of trying to stare her down, he spun around and stomped into the house.

"You, too," the old woman said to Sabrina. "Run upstairs and put on a bathrobe, then come back down. I could use your help with dinner."

The old "I need your help" routine, the girl thought as she plodded up the steps. Nine times out of ten, when an adult asked a child for help with something, it meant they were planning a lecture. Once she was out of her clothes and into a warm robe, she headed back downstairs, passing the bathroom door, where she could hear Daphne begging Elvis to get into the tub with her. A tremendous splash told Sabrina that the little girl had gotten her wish.

When she passed Puck's room, she heard a horrible smashing sound inside. Apparently, the idea of another bath was not sitting well with the Trickster King.

"Sabrina? Is that you, *liebling*?" Granny called when Sabrina came down the stairs.

The girl followed the voice and found the old woman in the kitchen, putting a pot of broth on the stove. Once it was in place, she turned to a cutting board and chopped carrots, onions, and celery into little pieces.

"What are we making?" Sabrina asked sarcastically. "Kangaroo-tail soup? Cream of fungus?"

"Chicken noodle," Granny replied. "Why don't you have a seat on that stool? I think it's time you and I had a talk."

Sabrina rolled her eyes but sat down.

"You've got a lot of anger in you, child," said Granny Relda.

Sure, she was angry! Who wouldn't be? She was tired of the secrets and the lies. Tired of the things hidden behind disguises, tired of the surprises that popped up every single day. No one in this town was what they seemed. One of them had her parents. Was she supposed to walk around making friends and passing out cookies?

"I get angry, too," her grandmother continued. "My son and daughter-in-law are out there somewhere, and I can't find them. Every night, after you girls are asleep, I ask Mirror to let me take a look at them. In a way, it makes me happy that they are still there, sleeping so peacefully, not even knowing all the trouble we're going through to find them, but a lot of times it just makes things worse.

"Some nights I crawl back into bed and I want to scream," Granny said, tossing the vegetables into the boiling broth. "I blame myself for not being able to find them. After all, there's more magic and books in this house than in ten thousand fairy tales combined, and yet I'm no closer to bringing them home today than I was a year ago.

"Sometimes I look around this town and wonder if the person responsible for all of our heartache is sitting next to me in the coffee shop," she continued. "Or maybe it's the lady behind me in line at the supermarket, or the woman who styles my hair at the beauty parlor. Maybe it's the nice man at the filling station who pumps gas into the car. Maybe it's the paperboy or the mailman or that girl who sells cookies for the scouts."

Sabrina's heart rate began to rise. Granny Relda felt exactly the way she did. Why hadn't she shared her true feelings about the Everafters? It would have kept her from feeling so guilty and confused about them. "I know how you feel," she said, encouraged by the old woman's revelations. "The Everafters can't be trusted."

"*Liebling*, that's not true," Granny said, setting down her knife. "Some of them are my friends. They are just like everyone else. They have families and homes and dreams."

"And murderous plots, kidnapping schemes, and plans to destroy the town."

"You don't really believe they are all bad, do you? What about Snow White and the sheriff?"

"We just haven't discovered what they're really up to yet."

"Sabrina!" Granny Relda reprimanded. "No grandchild of mine is going to be a bigot!"

"Bigot?"

"Yes, you're judging all of them by the actions of a few—that's bigotry, and it's hateful. I know it is difficult when you don't know who is responsible, but that doesn't mean everyone is guilty."

"I have a right to hate them! They took my parents away. How can you defend them?" Sabrina cried as she jumped off the stool.

"I will defend them and anyone else people choose to discriminate against. Yes, there are bad people among the Everafters, but there are bad people among us all. It's not fair to paint them all with the same brush."

The kitchen suddenly seemed so small, as though there wasn't room for the both of them anymore. Sabrina felt as if she were being suffocated.

"You can look at it any way you want," she said, taking a step backward. "But if they aren't all in on it, then they sure aren't stepping up to help. And every time you smile at one of them or shake one of their hands, you're just making it easier for them to stab you in the back."

"Sabrina," Granny said. "Take it from an old woman who knows. Anger grows like a weed. If you don't get ahold of it and pull it out, then it spreads and chokes you the rest of your life. Hate is a dangerous thing. If you cannot learn to control it, it will control you."

"I'll get ahold of my anger when my mom and dad are safe at home!" the girl cried. She spun around and rushed out of the room and up the stairs. She slammed the door of her bedroom and threw herself onto the bed. Burying her head under the pillows, she sobbed violently. In two weeks it would be Christmas, the second Christmas since one of them—one of the Everafters—had kidnapped her parents. Why didn't anyone care about bringing them home? Why was she the only one who saw the truth about the Everafters?

Sabrina awoke to a knocking on her bedroom door. She looked over at the clock on the nightstand and realized it was already seven o'clock at night. She had been asleep for more than three hours. Still in her robe, she crawled out of bed and opened the door. Mr. Canis was waiting on the other side.

"The family awaits you in the car," he said.

"I don't feel like going anywhere," she responded. The thought of seeing Granny Relda and Daphne right now made her sick to her stomach. They would just judge her again.

"Child, this is not an invitation," Mr. Canis said. "There is work to be done."

"Where are we going?"

Mr. Canis took a deep breath. "The answer to that question will not change the fact that you are going there."

Sabrina closed the door and got dressed, but the fresh clothes didn't do anything to hide the horrible odor coming off her skin. She'd slept through bath time and now smelled like a catfish, but she knew if she tried to clean up, she would have to face

Mr. Canis again. Once her sneakers were tied, she hurried through the empty house, put on her coat and hat, and opened the front door. Granny was waiting outside with her key ring in hand.

"Feeling better?" she asked.

Sabrina nodded. Thankfully, the old woman wasn't harping on their previous conversation.

"Good. A nap can do wonders for a person. Hurry along. Everyone else is in the car."

Daphne, Elvis, and Puck waited in the backseat, looking warm and well fed. The little girl and the dog both refused to look at her when she slid in beside them. They stared out the window and gave her the frostiest of cold shoulders. Puck, on the other hand, looked at her and laughed.

"You are in so much trouble." He chuckled, sounding impressed.

"Where are we going?" she asked again.

"The sheriff needs our help," Granny replied.

Mr. Canis steered through the country roads, heading toward the elementary school. When he got there, he pulled into the parking lot. Sheriff Hamstead's car was parked nearby, but the portly policeman was nowhere to be seen. Everyone piled out into the chilly air, and the old man once again climbed onto the roof of the car and sat in his meditative posture.

"If you need anything, please call for me," he said.

"Thanks, friend. I suspect this visit will have less drama than the last," Granny Relda said. "Elvis, stay in the car."

Elvis whined, not wanting to be left behind again.

"Buddy, you can come in with us, but there's a criminal stealing blankets out of the backseats of cars," Daphne warned. "He might snatch yours while we're inside."

The big dog bit down hard on the edge of his blanket and eyed the windows suspiciously as the family went into the school.

The Grimms made their way to the principal's office. There they found the sheriff sitting in a chair taking notes while Mr. Hamelin paced back and forth.

"What are they doing here?" the principal asked when the family stepped through the door.

"The sheriff asked us to come by," Granny explained.

"The Grimms are excellent at finding people," Hamstead said awkwardly. It was obvious to Sabrina he was trying to be discreet about the family being deputized.

"We're happy to help," Granny Relda said.

"No offense, Relda, but my kid is freezing out in the cold somewhere. I don't need an old woman and two kids; I need the police department," Hamelin said.

"I've got the best tracking dog in the world in the car," Granny said. "I'd take Elvis over a hundred police officers any day. We'll find your boy."

The principal sat down in his chair and rolled it over to the icy window. "It's so cold out there," he whispered.

"We were chasing Wendell this afternoon," Daphne said.

"I heard all about it," the man responded without turning away from the window.

"Then you know he's involved with the deaths," Granny said.

Hamelin angrily spun around in his seat and pointed his finger at the old woman. "He didn't do it!" he shouted.

"I'm in complete agreement. I've spoken to my girls and Ms. White, who was present at today's troubling event. I believe the boy is trying to stop the criminals responsible for this ghastly business."

Mr. Hamelin shook his head with frustration. "He's . . . One afternoon we watched an old black-and-white detective movie on TV together, and he was hooked. Now, everything's a mystery. I thought it was just a phase for him. I never suspected he'd get himself in trouble."

"So he's a detective, just like us?" Daphne asked.

"He also seems to have picked up his father's flair for music," Granny Relda said. "I hear a harmonica is his instrument of choice. He can control animals with it?"

Hamelin sank into his seat, looking defeated.

"Relda, he's a good kid," he said.

"I knew there was a reason I didn't like him," Puck mumbled.

Sabrina couldn't help but roll her eyes. A good kid wouldn't zombify a forestful of rabbits and send them chasing after children.

There was a knock at the door, and Mr. Sheepshank popped his head into the room.

"So sorry to interrupt," he said, pointing to the wristwatch on his freckled arm. "Mr. Hamelin, we have that meeting."

"Sheepshank, my son is missing!" the principal shouted angrily. Sabrina turned to look at the rosy-cheeked man, who smiled nervously.

"Of course. We can talk later," he said. He closed the door and was gone.

"Mr. Hamelin," Daphne said, "we don't want you to worry. We'll find your son and bring him back to you."

Granny Relda smiled at the little girl.

"Relda, I know I've had a history with your family. Henry and I traded a few punches back in the day, and Basil . . . well, he and I never saw eye to eye," the principal said.

"I like to think we're never too far along to start over," Granny said, extending her hand. Hamelin stared at it for a moment.

"You'll help me?" Hamelin asked, taking her hand and giving it a vigorous shake. "I think I had your family all wrong, Relda."

"We're Grimms, and this is what we do," Daphne said, then stood to shake Hamelin's hand, as well. Afterward she reached down, yanked on her belt, and pulled her pants up. Sabrina almost burst out laughing but quickly stopped herself when Sheriff Hamstead's angry face told her he recognized the little girl's impression. "Protecting and serving is how we roll."

"How can I help?" Hamelin asked.

"You can start with Wendell's locker number," Granny said.

The principal punched a key on his desktop computer, and the screen lit up. He typed in a few strokes and smiled.

"He's number three-two-three. That's right around the corner, near the boiler room door," he said. "Shall I show you the way?"

"No, please wait here," the sheriff said as he stood up from his chair. "We'll call you as soon as we know anything."

Hamstead and the family walked out of the office and down the hall until they found locker 323, right where the principal had told them it would be.

"Do you have some kind of magic that opens locks?" Sabrina asked as she eyed the combination lock on the door.

Granny opened her handbag and pulled out a hammer.

"I wouldn't call it magic, exactly," she said, handing the hammer to Puck. The boy grinned and raised the hammer high over his head. He brought it down hard on the lock, which snapped in two.

"Can I do another?" he asked, but the old woman snatched the hammer out of his hand and placed it back in her handbag. Then she tossed the broken pieces of the lock to the floor and opened the locker. Inside was Wendell's winter coat. Granny pulled it out and tucked it under her arm.

"I really appreciate this," the sheriff said. "One cop can't keep the peace in a town this size."

"Don't think twice about it," the old woman said.

Back in the parking lot, the Grimms and Puck found Mr. Canis where they had left him.

"We're heading into the forest," Granny said, opening the back door and letting Elvis out. "Why don't you stay here in case Wendell wanders back to the school?"

"Are you sure you won't be needing me?" the old man asked.

"We've got this one handled," Granny Relda replied.

"Can I ask you a question, Mr. Canis?" Daphne asked.

"Of course, little one."

"What do you think about when you're sitting on top of the car?"

Mr. Canis thought for a moment, then looked up at the moon, now high over the nearby forest. "I concentrate on all the people I hurt when I was unable to control myself."

"And that helps you stay calm?" Sabrina asked.

"No, child, but it gives me a reason to try," he replied.

Sabrina didn't know a lot of fairy-tale stories. Her dad used to say fairy tales were pointless. When other kids were reading about the Little Mermaid and Beauty and the Beast, her father was discussing the news with his daughters or reading them the Sunday comics using different voices for each character. Sabrina and Daphne did their fairy-tale reading on the sly or at school. Still, everyone knew the story of Little Red Riding Hood, and as Sabrina looked at Mr. Canis, a terrible realization ran through her. This man sitting on the car roof, who slept across the hall from them at night, had killed an old woman once upon a time. Only it wasn't a story; it had really happened. He had tried to eat a child, too. How could Granny let him live in the house?

Granny was holding Wendell's coat under Elvis's nose. The giant dog took a deep lungful and was soon trotting across the school lawn, sniffing madly in the grass.

"Looks like he's got the scent, *lieblings*," Granny said. "Let's go find our Wendell."

8

ELVIS SNIFFED THE AIR. GRANNY HAD SAID THAT once the big dog caught a scent, he never lost it. When he reached the edge of the trees, he stopped and barked impatiently at the family. It was obvious they were slowing him down. He sniffed wildly, rushing back and forth at the foot of a path, then barked again.

"Oh, I wish I could bottle his energy," Granny Relda said, taking Sabrina's arm to help get her across a fallen tree.

When they finally caught up with him, Elvis led the family into the forest. He sniffed wildly, darting off the path, only to return moments later with his nose glued to the ground. Sabrina heard a branch snap in the distance, and the dog's keen ears perked up. She expected him to run off howling in its direction, but instead he lowered his snout and continued to follow his invisible path.

Sabrina's feet crunched on the frozen ground. The night was

bitterly cold, and every once in a while she spotted snow flurries fluttering above her. She was freezing, even in her heavy coat. Poor Wendell was out here without even a jacket to protect him. If he was still alive, it was a miracle.

They walked for hours, calling out the boy's name and getting no response. Daphne said her toes were numb, and even Puck complained that they were wasting their time.

"The rabbits have turned on him," Puck insisted. "They're feasting on his chubby body as we speak."

"I promised Mr. Hamelin we would find his son," Granny said. "We're not going home until we do."

Luckily, they didn't have to look much longer. Elvis led them to a small clearing, where they beheld a sight so incredible, even Granny Relda gasped. A mound of fur nearly four feet high and six feet wide sat before them. At first, Sabrina thought it might be a bear, but as they got closer, they realized it wasn't a single animal but many. In fact, it was a pile of rabbits huddling together against the cold. Elvis barked at the pile, but the little forest animals paid him no attention. In fact, they acted as if he wasn't there at all.

"Elvis, are you telling us Wendell is at the bottom of this pile?" Daphne asked.

The dog sniffed the pile once more, then huffed.

"I told you!" Puck cried. "His woodland army mutinied! I hope he was delicious, little rodents!"

The old woman stepped close and leaned down. "Wendell!"

The mound stirred for a moment but then grew still.

"Wendell! Your father is worried sick about you," Granny Relda scolded. "Now come out of there this instant."

"No!" a muffled voice shouted from the depths of the rabbits. "You're going to send me up the river. I won't go."

"What does *send up the river* mean?" Daphne asked.

"He thinks we're taking him to jail," Sabrina explained.

"No one is sending you anywhere, Wendell," Granny said. "All we want to do is take you home."

The mound stirred. A brief note from the boy's harmonica was heard, and suddenly the rabbits rushed off in different directions, leaving the boy alone and lying on the ground. He looked perfectly fine to Sabrina. The rabbits had acted as a blanket, protecting him from the elements.

"Run, you dirty little carrot-munchers!" Puck shouted after them. "But know that your kind has made an enemy of the Trickster King!"

Granny stepped forward and helped Wendell to his feet, then wrapped him up in the coat she had taken from his locker.

"Would you like to explain what is going on, Wendell?" Granny asked.

"I didn't kill the janitor," he insisted.

"No one is saying you did."

"Though sending bunnies to eat us was not cool! I'm a seven-year-old girl," Daphne said. "Do you know how important bunnies are to me?"

"I didn't know if I could trust you. There are shady things going on at the school. I'm trying to stop it," the boy pleaded. "I couldn't risk getting caught. It would have ruined my investigation."

He shoved his hand into his coat pocket and pulled out a business card. He handed it to Granny. The old woman read it, looked impressed, and nodded at him.

"So you're a detective?" Granny Relda said with a smile.

Sabrina took the card and read it closely. It said, WENDELL EM-ORY HAMELIN, PRIVATE EYE. At the bottom of the card was a magnifying glass with a huge eye inside it.

Daphne snatched the card and studied it. "I want a business card, too."

"Wendell, we're detectives, as well," Granny said. "I suggest we share notes. You can tell us everything you know on the way back to school. Your father is a nervous wreck. He's waiting for us in his office."

The group trudged back through the forest, and Wendell told them all he had learned.

"I was leaving the school yesterday, when I looked back and saw something happening in Mr. Grumpner's room," he said, stopping to blow his nose into his handkerchief. "Sorry, I've got really bad allergies."

"How come you remember Mr. Grumpner?" Sabrina asked. "The rest of our class doesn't."

"My dad has a protection spell on our house. Whenever they dust the town, we aren't affected. Anyway, like I said, something crazy was happening in Mr. Grumpner's room. I peered through the window and saw him fall backward over some desks. At first I thought he was sick, but then I saw the monster."

"A giant spider?" Granny asked.

"Sort of," he said. "It had human body parts, too. It grabbed Grumpner and started covering him in its sticky web. I knew I had to do something. A private eye can't just let someone get roughed up. It's part of our code, but I'm not so great with the fisticuffs, you know?"

"Fisticuffs?" Daphne asked.

"Fighting," Sabrina explained.

"That's when I remembered something from science class about spiders—birds are their natural predators."

"What's a predator?" Daphne asked.

"It's like a hunter," Sabrina replied.

"So I did something I'd never done before. I got out a harmonica I'd bought and blew into it as hard as I could," the boy continued. "I didn't even know if it would work. Dad told me to never do it, on account of his past. Please don't tell him I bought the harmonica. He'll get real mad."

Granny took his hand. "Don't worry, Wendell."

He relaxed and continued. "I had no idea if I had the same ability as he does, but I had to try. So I just thought of birds, and before I knew it, the sky was full of them. They crashed through the window and landed at my feet. They were looking at me like I was their leader or something, like they were waiting for instructions, so I pointed at our teacher and said, 'Save Mr. Grumpner.'

"So, anyway, the birds attacked the monster. Unfortunately, it was too late."

"That explains the feathers," Daphne said.

"And what about the janitor?" Sabrina asked, still not sure she believed the strange boy's story.

"Ms. Spangler gave me a detention for refusing to play dodgeball," Wendell said. "When I walked in, there was this ugly, hairy thing fighting with Mrs. Heart and Ms. White. At first I thought it was a bear, but it moved way too fast, and it had these weird yellow eyes. Mrs. Heart was pretty useless against it. She hid behind a desk and screamed while Ms. White fought the thing. You should have seen her. For a dame, she's got quite a right hook."

"Dame?" Granny Relda asked.

Wendell blushed. "Sorry. I mean, for a teacher she's pretty tough. I got my harmonica out, wondering if I could control the monster like I had the birds, and at first it worked, but then it ran to the window, opened it, and leaped outside. When you guys founds us, I wasn't running away. I was trying to catch it."

"You're quite brave, Wendell," Granny Relda said.

"Being a private eye isn't for the faint of heart, Mrs. Grimm," he declared, wiping his nose on his handkerchief. "You have to have nerves of steel. All right, I've shared what I know. What have you three got to add to this caper?"

"We've had a run-in with an unusual creature, too," the old woman said. "A frog monster attacked us the other night."

"They have to be working together. It's too much of a coincidence. And why are they always at the school?" Sabrina asked. "I know I don't have any evidence to back this up, but I don't think these creatures are monsters. I think they may be Everafters—or rather, the children of Everafters, just like you."

"An excellent deduction," said Granny Relda. "And I suppose you've seen the dusty footprints all over the school."

The boy bit his lower lip. "Yes, I have. And, well, I wasn't going to say this, because I don't want to put you in any danger, but the dust isn't the result of bad custodial work. It's coming from the tunnels."

"Tunnels?" Sabrina and Daphne cried.

"Yes. I stumbled upon them the other day. Someone is digging underneath the school. The tunnels start in the boiler room and go on for miles."

"Could everything be connected—the tunnels, the giant spider, the hairy thing?" Daphne asked.

"Perhaps we should team up," Granny Relda said. "Combining our efforts might solve the case sooner."

"Sorry, lady, I work alone," Wendell said as they reached the front door of the school.

Sabrina rolled her eyes. *Someone's been watching too many detective movies, all right*, she thought.

"I understand," Granny said, trying her best to sound disappointed.

The moment they stepped into the school, Principal Hamelin came running in their direction. He swooped Wendell up in his arms and hugged him.

"Do you know how worried I have been?" his father said, half lecturing and half laughing.

"I'm sorry, Dad," the boy said. "But there's a caper afoot, and I'm in the thick of it."

"More detective nonsense? Wendell, I told you to give it a break!"

"Justice never takes a break, Dad," the boy said.

"Thank you, Relda," Mr. Hamelin said, reaching over and kissing the old woman on the cheek. "Thank you all."

Daphne tugged on her pants and stepped forward, mimicking the sheriff once again. "Just doing my job, citizen," she said.

The principal let the boy go, then reached his hand out to him. "Hand it over."

Wendell frowned. "But I need it," he argued. "It helps with my detective work."

"You're about to retire," his father said sternly. "C'mon, give it to me."

Wendell frowned, then reached into his pocket and pulled out his shiny harmonica. He reluctantly placed it in his father's hand and grimaced when Hamelin stuffed it into his suit pocket.

"I need to get him home," the principal said.

"Mr. Hamelin, I have a question," Sabrina said. "Are there any more children here at the school like Wendell?"

"What do you mean?" he asked.

"You know, children of Everafters?"

Hamelin took off his hat and scratched his head. "He's the only one I know about."

"Any other Everafters on the staff?"

Granny eyed Sabrina nervously. She was sure the old woman thought she'd say something mean about the Everafter community, but Granny didn't interrupt.

"Only Ms. White, myself, and now, of course, Mrs. Heart," he said. "About ten years ago Miss Muffet, the Beast, and the Frog Prince were teachers here, but they went in on a lottery ticket together and won millions of dollars. The next day, they all quit.

Can't say I can blame them, but it was a shame. Good teachers are hard to find."

"Of course," Granny Relda said. She looked at Sabrina, and the girl saw a sparkle in her eye, the kind her grandmother got when she found an important clue. "Well, we have to be going now."

"Thanks again, Relda. I owe your family a debt I have no idea how to repay," he said.

"We accept cash," Puck said.

Hamelin wrapped his arm around his son, and the two walked down the hall.

"We should check the tunnels now while no one is here," Daphne suggested, walking over to the boiler room door and trying the knob. "It's locked."

"That's probably for the best, *liebling*. If people are being killed to protect what's in those tunnels, I suggest we take the hint for now," Granny Relda replied. "In the meantime, I need to find a phone. If my hunch is right, I think I know the identity of our monsters—or at least their parents."

A skinny Christmas tree sat at the entrance to the police station. A few strands of tinsel and garland were wrapped sloppily around it. A couple of boxes of shiny bulbs sat underneath, waiting to be strung on the tree's dry, fragile limbs. As they passed the display,

Sabrina sympathized with the overworked sheriff. He didn't even have time to finish his holiday decorations.

Sheriff Hamstead was at the front desk, surrounded by six of the most unusual people Sabrina had ever seen. She recognized two of them immediately. Beauty and the Beast weren't a couple she would soon forget. The dazzlingly gorgeous Beauty was a complete contrast to her fur-covered, fang-faced husband. The others in the room, however, were complete strangers. She saw a pretty blond woman in a tiara and satiny blue gown standing next to a top-heavy strongman with enormous green eyes and an odd skin disorder; next to them was a chubby woman covered in jewels holding hands with—or in this case, holding the spindly leg of—an enormous black spider as big and fat as Elvis. Everyone was shouting at the sheriff.

"What's the meaning of this, Hamstead?" the Beast growled.

"We had dinner reservations at Old King Cole's!" Beauty cried. "Do you know how long it takes to get a table at this time of year? We planned this in September!"

The beautiful princess was as angry as anyone. "Drag me out of my home in the middle of the night," she huffed. "Do you realize my husband is the Frog Prince? We're royalty!"

"It's beyond rude," the prince complained.

The spider clicked angrily with its gigantic pincers.

"Settle down, everyone!" the sheriff shouted as he stood up and adjusted his pants. "Relda Grimm will explain everything."

The announcement caused everyone to shout even louder.

"Since when does Relda Grimm run the police force?" the lady with the spider demanded. Her eight-legged friend hissed in protest.

"The mayor has asked my family to help with the investigation of the two murders at Ferryport Landing Elementary," Granny replied.

The woman with the spider stamped her foot. "What's that got to do with us?" she asked.

"Miss Muffet, it has everything to do with you," the old woman replied. "And your husband and your child. In fact, it has to do with all your children."

The crowd gasped.

"None of us have children," the Beast declared.

"That's what I thought," Granny Relda said. "Until my granddaughter asked a question that I should have asked myself: 'Who else worked at Ferryport Landing Elementary?' I had nearly forgotten that you, the Frog Prince, and Little Miss Muffet were all teachers there before you all won the lottery."

Sabrina beamed with pride. Granny might have disapproved of Sabrina's suspicions about the Everafters, but it was those same suspicions that were helping solve the mystery.

"So we worked at the school. What does that have to do with the murders?" the Frog Prince croaked.

"Your former occupations aren't what's peculiar. It's your

retirement that's interesting. You see, none of you ever won the lottery," Hamstead replied.

Everyone gasped, even Puck.

"I called the state lottery commission," the sheriff said. "They have records of every lottery winner in the last fifty years. None of you are on their lists. So where did you get the money?"

The couples eyed one another for a long time before the Frog Princess broke down in tears.

"We were nearly broke when we found out I was pregnant," she sobbed. "All of our money was gone; we were worried we'd lose our house. If you go broke in Ferryport Landing, you stay that way. There's no one to bail you out. You can't move to another town. We would have been beggars in the street."

Beauty broke down, as well. "We were in the same predicament, barely making ends meet on Beast's teacher's salary. It was no way to raise a child. He told us he could help.

"One night, he brought over a spinning wheel and started spinning gold. I'd heard stories, but I'd never seen it happen. It was a miracle! By morning, we had enough to last us a dozen lifetimes. We sold it to a precious-metals merchant from New York City. We were rich overnight."

"Who spun the gold?" Sabrina said.

"Rumpelstiltskin!" the Frog Princess cried. The Frog Prince took her hand and begged her to be silent, but the tears and truth were already pouring out of her. "We had to come up with an explanation for the money, so we invented the lottery story."

"What did he want in return?" Hamstead demanded.

"He manipulated us!" Miss Muffet cried. "I don't expect you to understand, but it was like we weren't in control of our emotions. When we gave him the babies, we felt so desperate, so full of despair. Handing them over felt like the right thing for our children."

"You sold them?" Sabrina said. She had never heard a more horrible story in her entire life. "How could you sell your children?"

"It was like he crawled into our brains," the Beast said. "Afterward, the regret nearly killed us all, but at the time it seemed sensible."

Sabrina was so angry, she couldn't hold it back. "You filthy Everafters are nothing but animals! You would hand your own children over to a monster so you could cover yourselves in jewels and furs!"

Miss Muffet looked down at her sparkling necklace and started to cry. She ripped it from her neck and threw it into a nearby trash can.

"Sabrina," Granny said. "That's enough."

"I agree," Daphne said. "Take a chill pill."

Sabrina ignored them. "No wonder Wilhelm trapped you all in this town. You belong in a cage!"

"Sabrina Grimm, you will hold your tongue this instant!" Granny Relda ordered.

Sabrina was stunned. The old woman had never raised her voice to her. The girl's face was hot with embarrassment.

"You got yelled at," Puck taunted.

"Puck, that goes for you, as well!"

"We've never stopped looking for them," the Frog Prince said. "I'd give every penny of our fortune to get my daughter back."

"I believe they are closer than you think," Granny said. "If we showed you photos of all the children at the elementary school, do you think you could pick out which ones might be yours in their human disguises?"

"N-n-no, I don't think so," Beauty said, trying to control her sobbing. "We haven't seen them since they were a day old. We didn't even get to name them. Do you really think you've found them?"

Granny nodded grimly. "I do, but it's not entirely good news. Let me explain. Witnesses say there have been attacks by two so-called monsters on school grounds. One involved a giant spider. The second was a big, furry creature, and a third, which my family and I encountered ourselves, was a half-girl, half-frog creature."

"Wait—you think our children are involved in the murders?" Beauty said.

Granny nodded. "But if what you have told us about the day you gave them to Rumpelstiltskin is true, it's very likely they are being manipulated to commit these crimes."

"That's horrible! We have to get them away from him!" Miss Muffet cried.

"We will do our best to make that happen," Granny Relda said.

"You would do that for us?" the Beast asked.

"Of course," Daphne said proudly. "We're Grimms, and this is what we do."

Sabrina couldn't believe what she was hearing. These people were horrible. They'd sold their kids for money, and now Granny wanted to help get them back? They shouldn't be allowed within a hundred miles of a child.

"Do you need anything from me?" Hamstead asked the family.

"Actually, can I have a police hat?" Daphne asked the sheriff.

Hamstead smiled and nodded at the girl.

"You are so punk rock!" she cried.

Once the family was outside, Sabrina wasn't sure which was colder—the bitter winter air or Granny's attitude toward her. She also knew that Daphne was going to give her the silent treatment again. But it didn't matter to her anymore.

"I'm not sorry for what I said," she declared.

"Oh, we're well aware of that," Granny Relda said as they approached the car. Mr. Canis was waiting on the roof.

"I heard yelling," he said, crawling down to help the old woman into the front seat.

"I bet you're going to hear a lot more," Puck said, sounding hopeful.

"Everything is fine," the old woman said. "It is late, and I think we all need a good night of rest."

"Good idea," Daphne said. "We can search the tunnels tomorrow."

"No, I don't think so," Granny said as they got settled into the car. "Things have escalated to a point where I fear this case may be too dangerous. A few creepy Everafter children are one thing, but Rumpelstiltskin is another entirely. He's one of the most deranged and mysterious fairy-tale creatures who ever came to Ferryport Landing. I can't put you into harm's way when I have no idea what to expect."

"This isn't about danger," Sabrina said, shaking with anger and hurt. "We've been in plenty of dangerous situations since we moved to this town. This is about me, isn't it?"

Granny Relda turned in her seat and eyed the girl. "In the past, I thought you were smart enough to handle yourself. I thought you might possibly be the cleverest Grimm in the history of the family, but right now, I don't trust your judgment, Sabrina. You're not who I thought you were, child. I'm sorry, but this case is closed for the sisters Grimm."

Everyone was furious with Sabrina, so she crept upstairs to her room rather than hear another lecture. As she lay in bed, looking up at the model airplanes hanging from the ceiling, she contemplated life as the black sheep of the family. Days ago it would have seemed ideal. While everyone was busy solving mysteries, she could spend all her time searching for her parents. Unfortunately, she realized, Granny and Daphne needed her around more, not less, if only to remind them that they were living in a town full of people who wanted to kill them. Granny's trusting nature was bound to turn her into Ferryport Landing's next victim.

Daphne entered the room without a word, went to the dresser, and took out her pajamas. She changed in silence.

"Well, now we know what Granny's like when she's mad," Sabrina said.

Daphne gave her a look, but her lips were locked tight.

"Though I have to admit, I'm confused. She told us if we wanted to be good detectives, we had to look at every possibility," Sabrina said.

"You've got to get over this thing you have about Everafters," Daphne said.

"No, what I've got to do is convince everyone to stop being so naive," Sabrina said. "But let's just say I'm wrong about everything. Punishing us for my attitude isn't going to help solve the case. Granny can't do it all, and she's not going to get any help from Charming and the sheriff. We should be searching the tunnels. Who knows how far the bad guys have dug, or even what they're digging for? What if they're doing something really bad down there while Granny is running around trying to find out which of the kids at school are monsters?"

"So what do we do?"

"We do what we're supposed to do," Sabrina said. "We're Grimms, and something's wrong in this town. It's our job to find out what it is."

Once she was confident her grandmother and Mr. Canis were asleep, Sabrina shook her sister awake, and the two of them crawled out of bed. They crept out of their room and down the hall to Puck's bedroom.

"Don't step on the plate," Sabrina reminded her sister as she opened the door. Inside the boy's magical forest room, the sun had set, replaced by a sea of stars, each blinking brightly just for Puck. The boxing kangaroo was asleep in his ring. All was still except for the cascading waterfall splashing into the lagoon and the occasional roller-coaster car whipping along the track overhead.

The girls tiptoed along the path around the lagoon and then into some heavy brush. Eventually, they came to a trampoline, where Puck was lying sound asleep. The Trickster King wore a pair of baby blue footie pajamas that had little smiling stars and moons on them. Held close to his face was a soft pink stuffed unicorn with a rainbow sewn on its side. If only Sabrina had brought a camera, she could have also recorded his thumb in his mouth.

"Nice jammies." Daphne snickered.

"Wakie-wakie, eggs and bakie," Sabrina sang like she was waking an infant.

Puck stirred in his sleep but didn't wake. A big stream of drool escaped his mouth and ran down the front of his pajamas.

"Does someone have the sleepy-sleepies?" Daphne said, mimicking her sister's baby talk.

"Time to come back from dreamland, precious," the older girl said, shaking the boy roughly.

Puck sprang from his sleep with wings extended from his back. He waved his big pink unicorn like a deadly sword and slashed at the human children.

"What are you doing in my room?" he bellowed.

"I like Mr. Unicorn." Sabrina laughed. "Does he protect you from bad dreams?"

"His name is Kraven the Deceiver," Puck corrected before realizing what he was holding and who was with him. He tossed the stuffed animal aside and fluttered down to the ground.

"We've got a plan for tomorrow, and you're going to help us," Sabrina said.

"Forget it," the boy answered. "I don't want any part of this hero business. I'm telling the old lady to find another bodyguard for her stinky offspring. It's beneath me!"

"Such a shame, really. Our plan involves a lot of a mischief," Sabrina said.

Puck's eyes lit up. "I'm listening," he said.

"First, we need a few things from the Hall of Wonders," she said.

She led the children to Mirror's room, then reached into her pocket and took out her set of keys.

"Where did you get those?" Daphne asked.

"I've been borrowing the originals off Granny's key ring one by one and making copies at the hardware store," she explained.

"You've been stealing and lying!" Puck cried. "I'm so proud of you."

"Granny's going to be furious," Daphne said.

"I've been using them to try out magical stuff, things that might help us find Mom and Dad," she said, hoping the little girl would approve.

Daphne, however, grimaced and lowered her eyes.

Sabrina unlocked the door, and the trio stepped into Mirror's room and closed the door behind them. They hurried through the reflection and came out into the Hall of Wonders. Mirror was standing in front of his own full-length mirror, sucking in his plump belly and making muscle poses like a body builder.

"Doesn't anyone in this house sleep anymore?" he asked. "I suppose you're looking for help with your mother and father."

"No, this time we're actually working on a case, and we need some help," Sabrina said.

The little man smiled. "Very well, give me the details."

"We need something that will help us get through a locked door," Sabrina said. "Do you have something here that will let us walk through walls?"

"Or a wand that makes doors open?" Daphne asked.

"Or a flame thrower?" said Puck.

"Children, this isn't Walmart," Mirror replied. "I don't have everything, but there is something that might help. Follow me."

As they followed Mirror, Sabrina read the golden plaques on each of the doors, a favorite habit developed on previous visits: LEP-RECHAUN GOLD; FLOOR PLANS FOR GINGERBREAD HOUSES; SLEEPING POTIONS; TALKING FISH; GHOSTS OF CHRISTMAS PAST, PRESENT, AND FUTURE; TIK-TOK MEN; CALIBAN—the doors went on and on.

"How far does this hallway go?" Daphne asked.

"Miles," Mirror said.

"What's at the end?" Daphne asked.

"Something you don't want to mess around with, child," Mirror said, stopping at a door with a plaque that read THE PANTRY. He held out his hand, and Sabrina gave him her key ring. He searched through her collection and found the one that unlocked the door. Everyone stepped inside, where, much to the girls' chagrin, there stood an old, run-down refrigerator.

"I've never heard of a magic refrigerator," Daphne said. "Is that a Grimm story or someone else's?"

"There's no such thing as a magic refrigerator," Mirror said as he opened the door. "It's what's inside that's important."

He opened the fridge, bent down, and rummaged around inside, pulling out a bag of rotten carrots. "I really have to toss these out," he mumbled, then opened a carton of milk and took a sniff. His face crinkled up in disgust. Finally, he took out a package of juice boxes and handed them to the kids.

"Drink me," Daphne said as she read the brightly colored label aloud.

"These helped Alice," Mirror said. "They'll get the job done for you, too."

"Wait . . . are these from *Alice in Wonderland*?" Daphne asked.

"The original account is called *Alice's Adventures in Wonderland*," Mirror corrected.

"Sure, but will these make us shrink?" Sabrina asked.

"To about the size of an ant," Mirror said. "At that size you could just walk under the door and get into any room you want. But you'll need these, too." He reached into the fridge and pulled out several individually wrapped snack cakes covered in chocolate icing and promising a YUMMY CREAM FILLING. They looked just like the kind Sabrina used to buy at the deli near their Manhattan apartment, but the label read, EAT ME!

"These will make you big, but don't eat too many—they're not exactly Atkins friendly," Mirror warned. "Tweedledee and Tweedledum sold these for a week at their convenience store before your grandmother confiscated their stock. The town was filled with giant children. It took us a week to sort it out."

"We'll need four of each, I think," Sabrina said.

"But there's only three of us," Daphne pointed out.

"Once we're in the boiler room, we need a guide to the tunnels. The only person we know who has been in them is Wendell Hamelin. I think the great detective is going to change his mind about working alone," Sabrina replied.

The next day at school, the trio walked down the crowded hallway toward the boiler room. Sabrina scrutinized every kid along the way, wondering which one was a giant spider or a frog-girl. It was impossible to tell. The only thing she could be sure of was, they all looked exhausted, like they had been up all night.

Wendell was waiting for them with a handkerchief and a runny nose.

"I've been doing some thinking, and I believe that joining forces might be smart, but only under a couple of conditions," he said.

"What conditions?" Sabrina asked.

"Everyone stays behind me in case fisticuffs are necessary. Detective work is a dangerous business, and I don't need any dames getting hurt," the chubby boy said, puffing up his chest like a tough guy.

Sabrina rolled her eyes and fought off a laugh. "Fine," she said. "Us dames will let you handle any bad guys. I think we should have a look in the tunnels right away."

"I agree, but there's a problem," Wendell said, wiping his nose again. "They changed the locks on the boiler room door. I think they're on to us."

"Luckily, that's not a problem." Sabrina reached into her backpack and tossed the boy an Eat Me cake and a Drink Me juice box.

"What are these?" he asked.

"The key to the new lock," Puck said, clapping his hands and rubbing them eagerly.

"You want to do it now?" Daphne cried. "Ms. White will notice I'm gone and come looking for me."

"It's the perfect time," said her sister. "Lunch is too busy, and Granny Relda will be looking for us after school. We'll wait until the bell rings for class, and once the hall is empty, we'll get started."

Soon enough, the bell sounded, and the other kids filed into their classes. Sabrina, Daphne, Puck, and Wendell milled around, trying to appear as if they were on their way to class without actually going anywhere. Once they were alone in the hall, they took out their Drink Me juice boxes and inserted the handy straws attached to the sides.

"How much do we drink?" Daphne asked, sniffing at the box.

"I don't know," Sabrina said. "I guess until it starts working."

Puck took a long slurp, and when he was finished he opened his mouth and belched. "It's fruity!" he exclaimed. Suddenly, there was a loud, squeaky sound like a balloon losing its air, and Puck's body shrank to half its size. Even his clothes, the Eat Me cake, and the juice box got tiny.

"Drink more," Daphne insisted. "You aren't small enough to get under the door."

"And hurry up," Sabrina said, scanning the hallway. The last thing she wanted was a teacher or student to see this craziness.

Puck took another sip and shrank even further. Soon, he was no taller than a quarter standing on its end. Sabrina bent down and examined the tiny boy.

"You have no idea how tempted I am to squish you," she said.

"And you have no idea how big your nose hairs are," he squeaked.

Sabrina covered her face with her hand.

"Our turn," Daphne said. The three other children took big sips out of their boxes. The liquid did taste fruity, like pineapples and cherry pie at the same time. A cool tingle ran down Sabrina's throat, into her belly, and then into her legs and arms. The

sensation wasn't unlike having a good stretch after a wonderful night's sleep. A sudden shrinking followed. When she finished the box, she and the others were the same size as Puck.

"Let's get in there before we wind up on the bottom of someone's shoe," said the tiny Wendell. "I'll go first, in case there's something waiting for us on the other side."

He yanked out his hanky, blew hard on it, then shoved it back into his pocket. Then he walked underneath the door without even having to bend over. Daphne took Sabrina's hand, and together they followed, with Puck bringing up the rear.

"I should be doing the dangerous stuff," he grumbled.

Once the group was on the other side, the children had a chance to look around. The boiler room was dark and enormous. A gigantic bucket full of mops sat in the corner. Boxes of trash bags and rolls of toilet paper sat on a shelf that seemed miles above their heads. An ancient coal furnace rested in the center of the room like a monstrous robot from a Japanese cartoon. Not far off, a brand-new electric furnace clicked and popped as it pushed warm air throughout the vents of the school.

"Look at that table!" Daphne cried, pointing at a nearby desk. "It's huge."

Sabrina nodded in agreement.

"Look at that chair," Daphne said. "It's huge!"

Sabrina agreed.

"Look at that button!" Daphne said, running over to an enormous white button that had fallen off of someone's shirt. She tried to lift it, but it was too heavy for her in her shrunken state.

"It's huge!"

"We need to find you another word," Sabrina muttered.

"Hey! I'm seven! I don't know a lot of words," the little girl said.

"All right, rabbit boy," Puck said to Wendell. "Where's the entrance to the tunnel?"

"The lever that opens the entrance is in the old furnace," the boy detective said. "But it's way up there!"

"We need to eat the cakes and get big," Sabrina said.

The children reached into their pockets for their Eat Me cakes. Suddenly, the boiler room door opened.

"Someone's coming!" Sabrina shouted.

Through the door walked a man who seemed as tall as the giant Sabrina and Daphne had encountered when they first moved to Ferryport Landing, and for a moment the girls were lost in the memory of fighting it in the woods. They watched him close the door, then walk over to the coal furnace. He opened a small trapdoor on its side and reached inside, where he fiddled with something they couldn't see. Sabrina guessed it was a lever or button of some kind, because a hum filled the room, and the coal furnace slid across the floor to reveal a secret hatch beneath it.

"That's my dad," Wendell whispered, his eyes confused and a little worried.

Sabrina craned her neck to look into the giant's face. It was indeed Principal Hamelin, but what was he doing?

The principal waited patiently until the secret hatch was completely revealed, then descended a flight of stairs until he could no longer be seen.

"What's your father doing?" Sabrina asked Wendell.

"I don't know, but we have to follow him," he said, taking off like a shot in a sprint toward the hatch.

"Wait!" Sabrina cried, but the boy detective ignored her. The rest of the children were forced to chase after him. When they finally caught up with him, he was already trying to open his Eat Me cake.

"Wait a sec. Maybe this isn't a good idea," Sabrina said.

"I need to know if he's involved in this," Wendell said.

"But maybe you don't want to know," Sabrina said.

Wendell paced back and forth, clearly unsure of what to do next. Then he stopped and stared down into the hatch.

"No, if he's involved in this, I have to stop him," he said. "I can't just look the other way because he's my dad."

"Wendell, this isn't one of those old detective movies you watch," Sabrina said. "This is real life. You might not like what we find down there."

"Justice has to be served," Wendell said.

"We should eat the cakes if we're going to tackle these steps," Daphne said, looking down into the hatch. "At this size, we'll break our necks if we fall."

"But if we go down there at our normal sizes, he's sure to spot us," Sabrina argued.

"No worries, girls. I have a brilliant plan," Puck said proudly. He spun around on his heels and transformed into an elephant, albeit a tiny one. He let out a mighty roar and charged off into the shadows of the room.

"Puck, we don't have time for your stupidity!" Sabrina shouted after him, but the boy-elephant did not respond. Soon she could hear the scraping of metal on the floor. When elephant Puck returned, he was pushing a dustpan with his trunk, all the way to the edge of the steps. When the pan was on the edge of the top step, the elephant morphed back into the boy.

"Get in," he said.

Sabrina looked at the dustpan hanging precariously over the edge and quickly understood Puck's "brilliant" plan.

"No way," she said. "We'll kill ourselves in that thing."

"You'll be fine," Puck assured Sabrina. "You'll probably need someone to feed you for the rest of your life, but you'll make it. Stop being a baby and get in."

Daphne was already climbing inside. "We survived Granny's driving," she said. "We'll survive this, too."

Sabrina looked at Wendell. He shrugged, and the two of them climbed into the dustpan.

"I suggest you stay in the back of this thing," Puck said with an excited giggle. "Oh, and one more thing . . ."

"What?" Sabrina cried. She didn't like the tone of his voice.

"Buckle up, kiddies!" Puck shouted as he walked to the edge of the pan and leaped into the air. His body came down hard, and the back of the pan tilted high into the air, sending the whole thing sliding down the steps like a bobsled. With each step it cleared, the dustpan increased in speed, until finally it crashed at the bottom of the stairs. Several minutes later, Sabrina stopped screaming. Then she got up and punched Puck in the arm.

"Hey, I got us here, didn't I?" he complained as he rubbed his sore shoulder.

The children climbed out of the dustpan and headed down a long, cavernous hall carved out of stone. The floor was covered in dust, and they left tiny footprints behind them. Along the rocky path were pickaxes and dusty shovels, old buckets, and miles and miles of rope.

What are they up to down here? Sabrina wondered as they continued onward. The tunnel occasionally broke off into rooms, but many of them were blocked by cave-ins.

When the children reached a fork in the tunnel, they stopped.

"Which way should we go?" Daphne asked.

"I can't say. This is as far as I have gone," Wendell said.

Sabrina heard voices arguing in the tunnel to the left.

"Listen! There's someone else down here with your father," she said.

"Let's find out who," Wendell insisted, so they followed the tunnel to the left, in the direction of the shouting. It took forever in their tiny state, but they crept along as best they could, finally moving close enough to see two figures in the dark. One was clearly Principal Hamelin, his face illuminated by a burning torch mounted on the wall, but the other person was drowned in shadows and unrecognizable.

"This has gone too far. No one was supposed to die," Hamelin said. He was wringing his hands angrily.

"Tiny distractions, Piper. The biggest threat to our success has been your lack of commitment," his partner said in a creaky voice. To Sabrina, the mysterious figure sounded like he was a thousand years old and hadn't had a sip of water in just as long. "We would have already reached our goal if not for last night."

"My son was missing!" Hamelin cried.

"I understand, Piper, believe me," the voice crackled. "I'm a father, too. The difference is that my children have been raised to understand how important our work is to the future of our community, while your child's meddling has drawn unwanted attention and puts this plan at risk. If you would just let me have a talk with him, I know I could persuade him to help us."

"Stay away from my son," the principal growled. "I don't want you playing with his head."

"Suit yourself. Our partnership is almost over, anyway. Tonight we push forward. Success is close at hand. That is, if you can find the time to make it happen."

Hamelin's voice was so angry, it shook. "Don't question my dedication. This was my idea, after all."

"I'm glad to see you still remember."

"No more deaths," Hamelin demanded.

"We'll do our best," the figure said. "Now, I believe you have a school to run. It's best to keep things running smoothly. We don't want to have to deal with any prying eyes or difficult questions."

"I know how to do my job," Hamelin snapped. He spun around and rushed back up the tunnel, nearly stepping on his own son, who managed to leap out of the way just in time.

"Are you OK?" Daphne asked, taking Wendell's hand in her own.

"I can't believe it," the boy said. His eyes looked lost.

"We should go farther into the tunnel," Sabrina suggested. "We need to know why they're doing all this digging. Whatever this is all about, it happens tonight!"

"Sabrina's right," Wendell said. "Let's keep going."

"Or . . . maybe we just run out of here screaming for our lives," Puck said, his voice shaking.

"Huh? Why?" Sabrina asked.

Puck pointed into the dark just as something crawled out of it. An enormous brown mouse that seemed as big as a semitruck lumbered toward them. Its pink nose and whiskers flicked and twitched as it sniffed at the children. Sabrina knew that at their current size, they probably looked like a great snack for the hungry mouse.

"Unwrap the cakes," Sabrina whispered, eyeing the mouse. "Slowly."

The children did as she suggested, and everyone was just about to put the cakes in their mouths when the mouse let out a roar and barreled forward. Surprised, Sabrina fell backward as the mouse charged toward her. Daphne screamed, and Puck leaped into the path of the mouse to drag Sabrina to her feet. Unfortunately, she dropped her cake in the fall. The mouse spotted it, sniffed it, and, with a quick flick of its tongue, ate it.

"Oh, man," Puck said, quickly shoving his own little chocolate cake into his mouth, "this is going to be awesome."

"That was bad, wasn't it?" Sabrina said sheepishly.

Puck offered Sabrina his pinky.

"Hang on, Sabrina," Puck said, flashing his devilish grin. "This is about to get interesting."

Sabrina grabbed Puck's finger as she heard the sound of a balloon inflating and watched the first changes affect the mouse's body. A ripple rolled across its skin. Its eyes widened as its body grew by a thousand times, yet its little legs and head stayed the exact same size, causing its massive body to crash to the ground. This was followed by a loud, squeaky rubber sound as the rodent's feet, legs, and head grew to match the rest of its body. The rest of the transformation was lost to Sabrina as Puck grabbed her by the arms and dragged her away down the tunnel.

There was another inflation sound, and Sabrina was yanked off the ground. Puck's legs shot upward like skyscrapers, pushing him to his normal height. Sabrina dangled from his pinky, looking down at the dizzying drop below her. Puck's upper body and hands finally followed, and his pinky got thicker. Sabrina held on with all her might. Luckily, Puck was paying attention. He quickly swung her into his shirt pocket, where she clung to the top, just as Puck's head inflated.

Meanwhile, Daphne and Wendell were changing, too. The little girl's head and feet were the first to inflate, and Daphne hopped around like a pumpkin with shoes trying to escape from its patch.

"I don't like this at all," she groaned. Her legs sprouted up like overeager cornstalks, followed by her upper body, and lastly her neck. Wendell experienced the same kind of disturbing growth.

"It's all good," the runny-nosed detective announced, checking for all ten fingers as the children ran. Sabrina, however, didn't think things were "all good." The mouse was getting bigger and bigger until it was nearly as wide as the tunnel, and, worse, it seemed very, very angry.

Puck giggled louder with every step. When they reached the steps that led to the boiler room, he helped Daphne up, and Wendell followed behind them. When they got to the top, they raced across the room to the door, unlocked it, and hurried into the hall, where Puck was laughing so hard, he could hardly breathe.

"What is so funny about this?" Sabrina shouted.

The boy looked down into his pocket. "What are you squeaking about? We got away safe and sound, didn't we?"

He had barely finished his sentence when the door flew off its hinges, slammed against the opposite wall, and fell heavily to the floor. The giant mouse lumbered into the hallway. It was as big as a stuffed buffalo Sabrina had once seen at the Natural History Museum, but it let out a deafening squeak and licked its gigantic front teeth.

"Well, Wendell, you wanted to do the dangerous stuff." Puck laughed. "Be my guest!"

"All right, everyone," Wendell said. "It might be big, but it's still a mouse, and it's probably more afraid of us than we are of it. If we stay calm, it won't attack."

The school bell rang, and every classroom door opened. The hallway was immediately flooded with a sea of noisy children, eager to get to their next class. The mouse stomped hard, creating a chasm in the shiny floor, and all conversation ended abruptly.

"What's plan B?" Daphne asked.

9

O K, EVERYONE, THERE'S NO NEED TO PANIC. We're professionals, and we know how to handle things like this," Daphne assured the crowd of stunned students as she flashed her shiny badge.

All at once, every kid at Ferryport Landing Elementary freaked out. They screamed and ran toward every available exit. Some raced into classrooms, barricaded the doors with desks, and climbed out windows.

Puck peered into his pocket and smiled at Sabrina.

"Hang on, I've got this," he said, flashing her a grin. He spun around on his heels and transformed into an orange-and-white alley cat. Sabrina found herself clinging to the cat's ear as it charged toward the giant mouse. Once he was close enough, Puck the cat hissed aggressively. Suddenly, what Sabrina could only describe as a smile crept across the mouse's face. It leaned its massive head down to the cat, opened its mouth, and roared angrily. Puck's short, tabby hair was blown back as if he were standing in a heavy wind, and Sabrina nearly flew off his ear. The cat backed away and transformed into a boy again.

"It was worth a try!" Daphne shouted.

"Don't worry," Puck said, with Sabrina back inside his shirt pocket. "I've got a million more ideas where that one came from." The boy spun around to face the mouse, and his wings popped out of his back. Flapping strongly, he soared over the mouse and landed on its back.

"Yee-haw!" he cried, jabbing his heels into the mouse's side. The giant rodent squealed in pain, lifted itself on two legs, and kicked wildly, causing Puck to bounce around like a rodeo cowboy. Sabrina was tossed around mercilessly inside his pocket.

In an effort to lose its rider, the mouse slammed into walls, broke down doors, and put some serious dents into a row of lockers. It shattered a trophy case, sending glass, track medals, and baseball trophies skittering down the hallway. It crashed into a banner announcing the library's bake sale and ripped it off the wall.

Of course, Puck laughed with every violent buck of the mouse's hind legs.

"Puck, cut it out!" Sabrina shouted, clutching the top of the pocket. But she knew the boy couldn't hear her over the commotion he was making.

Daphne rushed across the hallway, avoiding the mouse's flapping tail. She reached into her pocket and pulled out her half-full Drink Me juice box and aimed it at the mouse's mouth.

"Daphne, you're a genius!" Sabrina cried.

Daphne wound up like a big-league pitcher, waited for the mouse to open its gaping mouth, and tossed the juice box as hard as she could. Unfortunately, instead of slipping down the mouse's throat, the box bounced off one of its gnarly yellow teeth and fell to the ground. The mouse flattened the box with a stomp, spraying juice all over the hallway.

"We're just making it mad!" Wendell shouted.

The boy was right. The mouse bellowed angrily, then headed toward the exit door. Unfortunately, Daphne was right in its path.

"Run!" Sabrina yelled, but there was no way the little girl could move that quickly. Luckily, Wendell was there, and he pushed Daphne to safety just as the enormous rodent lumbered past them like an out-of-control train. It crashed through the exit doors, breaking them off their hinges, and charged outside.

Puck laughed the whole way, until a low-hanging tree with a thick limb knocked him off his ride. He fell hard on his back, sending what was left of his Drink Me juice box flying. The fall launched Sabrina out of his pocket and onto the lawn several yards away. By the time she got her bearings, the mouse was already on top of Puck, doing what it could to sink its sharp teeth into him.

"Juice!" Puck demanded, as Daphne and Wendell raced to his side. Puck snatched Wendell's Drink Me juice box with a free hand and squeezed its contents into the mouse's mouth until the box was crumpled and empty. Almost immediately, a ripple ran across the mouse's skin. The rodent shrank rapidly until it was once again a little brown mouse, sitting on the boy's chest.

Puck looked down at it and laughed. Then he ran his finger over the mouse's coat. "Good try," he told the rodent. "You almost had me."

Daphne helped Puck to his feet.

"Where's Sabrina?" she asked.

"Don't worry, marshmallow, she's right here in my pocket," Puck said as he looked inside. "Uh-oh."

"What's *uh-oh*?" Daphne cried.

"She's not in there," Puck said.

The little girl's eyes got as big as saucers.

"Don't anyone move," Wendell said. "She probably fell out here on the lawn, and we could step on her."

"Sabrina!" Daphne shouted.

"I'm here!" Sabrina yelled, waving her hands and jumping up and down, but none of the children could see or hear her amid the grass that towered over her head.

"What if we've already stepped on her?" her sister cried as tears streamed down her face.

"Let's check," Wendell said. He slowly lifted each of his shoes. "She's not on mine."

Puck slowly looked under his sneakers. "All clear!"

Daphne checked one foot and then the next. A big smile of relief came to her face.

"I think we'd better get the old lady," Puck said as his wings sprouted. "Best that I fly us out of here so we don't squish her."

In a few moments he had snatched the other children off the ground, and they were all flying away. Sabrina watched them disappear into the horizon.

"Don't you dare leave me!" she screamed, knowing that they couldn't hear her. She looked around at her strange environment. The school was only steps away for a normal-sized person, but for her it was much more trying. Staying put was probably the smart idea, but the air was freezing, even with her coat on, so she shoved her hands into her pockets and marched toward the entrance to the school.

The walk took forever, but finding somewhere safe and warm to rest was now Sabrina's main priority. She remembered that the heat in Mr. Sheepshank's office was always on full blast, and she was less likely to get trampled there than if she headed for a classroom. When she finally got to the front entrance and climbed the steep wheelchair ramp, she ran down the hall and made her way to the main office door. She'd hoped it would be a safe place to hide until Puck could return with her grandmother, but as soon as she crawled underneath the door, she knew she had even bigger problems.

"There's another roach!" the secretary with the big glasses cried. She reached into a drawer and pulled out an aerosol spray can, shook it vigorously, and got up from her desk. One glance at the can told Sabrina all she needed to know about what was going to happen next. It didn't take a rocket scientist to understand what ROACH-BE-DEAD meant.

She ran frantically along the rug, racing under the secretary's desk just as the gigantic woman rounded the other side. When Sabrina came into the light, the other secretary was there, chomping on a sandwich. She mumbled loudly and pointed at tiny Sabrina, causing the first secretary to come back around. The girl dashed under the desk again, but this time the secretary got down on her knees, pointed the spray can at her, and pushed the nozzle. This was unbelievable. A giant mouse had just rampaged through the school, and these goofy secretaries were worried about roaches? Sabrina braced for a coating of poison and, most likely, a horrible death, but luckily the nozzle was pointed upward, and the spray landed all over the desk.

"This one's fast." The first secretary scowled.

"Don't send it running over here!" the second secretary cried. "Those things give me the heebie-jeebies."

Sabrina darted behind a file cabinet.

"Where did it go?" the first secretary groaned. "Oh, I've got you now!"

Sabrina's safe hiding place began to rock back and forth.

"I'm not a cockroach!" she shouted, but she knew the woman couldn't hear her. A stream of the poison came showering down from above. Sabrina darted out of the way, but the secretary seemed to anticipate her escape route and was waiting for her on the other side. The girl looked up to find the nozzle of the can pointing right at her.

But the secretary never got a chance to finish her deadly work. The office door opened, and Mr. Sheepshank entered.

"Hello, ladies. The commotion is all over."

"What was it?" the secretary with the roach spray asked.

"Oh, just a big dog some kid let in," he replied. "Scared everybody half to death. Most of the kids have already left for home. Principal Hamelin just told me to let you two go, as well."

"Early dismissal for the grown-ups? I love it!" the secretary with the roach spray cheered. She quickly forgot about Sabrina and got to her feet.

Sabrina cowered as the women packed their things and left. When they were gone, Sheepshank closed the door and shuffled into his office. When Sabrina's heart stopped beating like it was trying to get out of her chest, she found a warm spot on the rug and sat down. Before she knew it, she had fallen fast asleep.

୧୬

Sabrina woke up inside Elvis's nose.

"Did you find something, boy?" Granny asked.

"I believe he has," Mr. Canis said.

With her head covered in dog boogers and mucus, Sabrina kicked for freedom, but this only caused the dog to snort deeply, and she rocketed into his nasal cavity, slid down his throat, and was quickly coughed out onto the office floor.

Dazed, Sabrina got to her feet and found Granny Relda peering down at her through a magnifying glass.

"Hello, young lady," she said as she reached into her handbag and removed a Drink Me juice box. A moment later, she was as tiny as Sabrina. She held two Eat Me cakes in her hand and a world of anger in her eyes. Her round face and button nose were so red with frustration, Sabrina wondered if smoke might blow out of her ears.

"Granny, you won't believe what I found out," Sabrina said, hoping her news would change the old woman's mood.

"I agree, Sabrina," Granny Relda snapped. "I doubt I'll believe anything you say for a very long time."

"Daphne told you about the keys?"

"She didn't have to," Granny said as she handed Sabrina a cake. She unwrapped her own and took a big bite. Sabrina did the same, and together the two of them sprouted up to their normal heights.

Unfortunately, Elvis's boogers grew at the same rate. The Great Dane looked disgusted at the goo that covered Sabrina from head to toe.

Daphne, who was standing nearby, ran to hug her sister but halted when she saw the disgusting mess that covered Sabrina. "I'm sorry. I love you, but you are way, way too gross," the little girl said.

"We got into the boiler room," Sabrina said, still hoping to impress her grandmother.

"She knows," Puck said sheepishly. He and Wendell leaned against the wall, looking guilty.

Why wasn't everyone excited? They had found an important clue.

"I also know you did it by breaking almost every one of my rules," Granny lectured. "I suppose you are proud of yourself?"

"You told us that kind of thing was our responsibility," Sabrina argued. "The whole 'We're Grimms, and this is what we do' baloney. Now that we're actually trying, you want us to stop."

"I think you know that sneaking around behind my back, copying my keys, testing out magic and potions in the middle of the night, and dragging your sister into danger is hardly what I meant," said Granny. "Add to that your lousy attitude about Everafters, and I just don't see you as much of a help right now."

Sabrina's eyes welled with tears, but she refused to cry. She bit her lip hard and squeezed her fists tight. The last thing she would do was show the old woman that her words had stung.

Granny Relda reached out her hand. "Hand them over," she said.

Sabrina recoiled as if the old woman were handing her a snake. "I need them!" she cried.

"You are not responsible enough for your own set," the old woman said. "If you were, you would have asked for them rather than steal mine and copy them."

"Someone has to look for my parents!" Sabrina shouted.

"Give them to me, Sabrina," the old woman insisted.

Sabrina reached into her pocket and placed the keys in her grandmother's hand. "You don't care if we ever find them, do you?" she asked.

"Sabrina!" Daphne cried.

The old woman ignored her question. Instead, she dropped the keys into her handbag and shut it tight.

"Come along, Mr. Canis. We should get the children home. I believe they are all in need of a hot meal," Granny said.

Dinnertime was quiet. No one talked, no one made eye contact, and no one smiled. Even Puck, who could usually be counted on to fart during dinner, was oddly silent. Afterward, Granny washed the dishes while Puck, Sabrina, and Daphne stared into their laps.

Elvis eyed Sabrina from time to time but kept his distance—most likely because of her time inside his nose.

A knock at the door broke the silence. Granny Relda rushed to open it and found Snow White standing outside in the cold. The old woman quickly invited her into the house.

"Thank you so much for coming, Snow," Granny said as she took off her apron and folded it.

"I'm happy to help! I'll take any chance to spend some time with my favorite student," the teacher said.

"That's me!" Daphne cried as she rushed to the door.

"What's going on?" Sabrina asked.

"Mr. Canis and I are going to investigate what is underneath the school," Granny Relda replied. "While we're gone, Ms. White will be looking after you."

"You got us a babysitter?" Sabrina cried indignantly. "I'm too old for a babysitter."

"You're too old?" Puck said to her. "I'm more than four thousand years old. This is an outrage!"

"I might have thought the same thing this morning," Granny replied as she put on her coat.

Just then, a car-horn blast came from outside.

"That's the sheriff," Mr. Canis announced as he descended the steps. He opened the closet and took out his and Granny Relda's coats.

"We should go," Sabrina fumed. "We've seen the tunnels. We know how to get down into them."

"Oh, we've got a guide," Granny replied.

There was another knock at the door, and when Mr. Canis opened it, Wendell Hamelin stepped inside. He was wearing a long trench coat and had a fedora pulled down over his face, like he had stepped out of a detective novel.

"You're taking him?" Sabrina cried.

Granny ignored her.

"The sheriff says we'd better get going," the boy said, wiping his runny nose on his handkerchief. He looked nervous and sad about the night's activities.

"Wendell, you don't have to come with us," Granny said. "Your father is caught up in this. I wouldn't blame you for wanting to stay home."

"No, I have to go. He didn't come home from work tonight, so I didn't get a chance to convince him to stop whatever it is he's doing down there," Wendell said. "He's my dad. I have to try to change his mind."

Granny Relda, Mr. Canis, and Wendell said their good-byes and were soon gone, leaving Sabrina standing by the door with a stunned expression on her face.

"Well, now . . ." Snow White said uncomfortably, reaching into her handbag and pulling out a board game. "Who wants to play Candy Land?"

Snow White did her best to keep the kids busy. She set up the board game, but Puck had no patience for it. When he landed on Molasses Swamp and lost a turn, he flew into a rage, flinging the board and all the pieces out the front door and into the yard. Later, after he had calmed down, Ms. White suggested they play charades. Once again, Puck was the spoiler, acting out the names of tree gnomes and pixies who had lived three hundred years ago and insisting they were as famous as any astronaut or president. Eventually, even Snow White gave up and let the children do what they really wanted to do—research.

The girls searched the library for titles that might be of help. With half their family traipsing around in dark tunnels, Sabrina and Daphne felt the least they could do was make sure that nothing was overlooked. Eventually, Sabrina came across her great-aunt Matilda's pamphlet, the one entitled *Rumpelstiltskin's Secret Nature*. She could see it was going to be a dry read, but it might have clues that could help. Besides, her curiosity about the child-buying weirdo was impossible to resist. She fell into a chair and started on page one.

Rumpelstiltskin's story was a famous fairy tale; everyone knew it, but after nearly a month in Ferryport Landing, Sabrina had learned not to assume anything when it came to Everafters. It seemed as if all the bedtime stories she had heard and movies she had seen about the various residents of her new hometown were always wrong, sometimes missing a lot of important details. Best to learn from her ancestors what the true story was.

Matilda Grimm's research was meticulous. Sabrina was shocked to see how much information her great aunt had packed into the little pamphlet. It looked as if months of work had gone into analyzing every single nuance of Rumpelstiltskin's personality, powers, and actions. Matilda had theories on how he spun straw into gold, where he came from, and why he tricked people out of their children.

The book also retold at least two dozen versions of the original tale. The story Sabrina knew involved a woman who begged Rumpelstiltskin for his help. In exchange, she promised to give him her firstborn child. When the baby finally arrived, the woman demanded a chance to keep it, so Rumpelstiltskin wagered that she would never be able to guess his real name. Of course, by the end of the story, she had figured it out, making the little man so angry, he actually ripped himself in two. But Matilda said there was an alternate version of the ending that not many people knew. In the other ending, Rumpelstiltskin didn't rip himself in half—he actually blew up like a bomb, killing everyone within a mile.

One chapter, entitled "The Power of Rumpelstiltskin," contained theories on the source of the little man's powers. Matilda believed he absorbed energy, which made him a walking battery, and he converted that energy into explosive power. Unfortunately, the more of Matilda's theories Sabrina read, the more questions arose.

"It doesn't make any sense!" Sabrina cried. "What do Rumpelstiltskin, the Pied Piper, the children of Everafters, and a bunch of tunnels under the school have in common?"

"The barrier," Puck replied.

"What?" Sabrina asked.

"The barrier runs very close to the school," Puck said. "You do remember making me crash into it, don't you?"

"You're just telling me this now?" Sabrina cried.

"Seemed obvious to me," the Trickster King replied.

"They're digging to the barrier," Daphne said.

"But what would be the point?" Snow asked.

"The point is, the magic might not be as powerful underground," Sabrina said.

"All right, kids, calm down," Snow White said. "Even if the barrier is weaker, they'd still need a huge magic explosion to crack it open."

"They've got one," Sabrina said, holding up her great-aunt's pamphlet. "Rumpelstiltskin is a walking bomb. When he loses his temper, he can blow up a whole town. He and Hamelin are working together! They're going to blow a hole in the barrier."

"But that's insane. The river is on the other side of the barrier—at least in that part of town. Even if you could crack it open, the water would drown you," Snow White pointed out. "Besides, from what I hear, bedrock, which is nearly impossible to dig through, rises up under the river. You'd need an army of miners to get through it, and this town isn't exactly full of people willing to do that kind of backbreaking work."

"They don't need willing miners if they have unwilling ones!" Sabrina cried. "We know the principal can control rats. Maybe he's using them to chew through the rocks."

"That's stupid!" Puck said.

"You're stupid!" she shouted back.

"Maybe he's not using rats," Daphne said uncomfortably.

"What else could he use?" asked Snow.

Daphne raced to the bookshelf, searched through the titles, and came back to the table with a thick book written by their distant relatives, Jacob and Wilhelm. She flipped through the pages furiously until she stopped on a story called "The Pied Piper of Hamelin."

"I think we'd better read this," she insisted.

Snow pulled the book into her lap and read the story from beginning to end. What they learned surprised everyone. The famous story of the piper who hypnotized an army of rodents and then drove them into the sea had a lot of twists and turns. Hamelin drowned the rats, but he didn't do it to be a hero. He did it for a paycheck. In his day, he used to travel from town to town, using his pipes to clean up messes. He drove the spiders out of Paris, the monkeys out of Bombay, and the snakes out of Prague. But he did it for money. When he showed up in the little Austrian town of Hamelin, the townspeople were eager for his help with their vermin infestation.

"What's *vermin* mean?" Daphne asked.

"Rats and mice," Sabrina explained.

"Rats were everywhere," Ms. White continued. "They spread a lot of disease, and people were getting sick. Everything the town tried failed. So the piper agreed to handle their problem, but that wasn't the end of the town's difficulties. When the piper came back, he wanted payment, but the town refused. They swindled him, and he was furious."

"What happened?" Sabrina asked, already sensing the story's unhappy ending.

"He gave them twenty-four hours to come up with the money, but they just laughed at him. So he blew into his bagpipes, and the town's children congregated around him. The piper marched out of town, with the children following behind him—just like the rats. Their families tried to stop them, but reports say the kids were in a trance and kept on following the music. They were never seen again."

"So of course it makes a lot of sense to hire him to be principal of an elementary school!" Sabrina said angrily.

"Rats or brats," Puck said. "What's the difference?"

Suddenly, the truth dawned on Sabrina. "He's hypnotizing the students. That's who's digging the tunnels!" she cried.

"What are you talking about?" Daphne said.

"You've seen the kids at school. They're exhausted. It's because they've been working all night. The Piper has been using his magic to make them work, and now that they've reached the barrier, it's Rumpelstiltskin's turn to blow the place sky high. We have to warn Granny!"

"The sheriff and Mr. Canis are with her," the teacher replied. "She's very smart. She'll figure this all out before anyone gets hurt."

"What if she doesn't?" Puck asked.

Sabrina was surprised. The boy usually acted as if he didn't care about anyone but himself. "If Rumpelstiltskin blows a hole in the barrier," Puck continued, "the walls will collapse on everyone inside the tunnels, and the river will sweep them away!"

Now Sabrina was stunned. "Since when did you become a hero?"

"Hero? I just want to see it happen," Puck said. "It'll be hilarious!"

Snow White looked from child to child and then reached for her car keys.

"Get your coats on," she said.

"We're going to the tunnels?" Daphne asked.

"Yes, but if I think it's too dangerous, we'll turn right around."

Soon they rushed out the front door, only to have Snow White crash into Mayor Charming, who was coming up the path at that very moment.

"Snow," Charming said, surprised, "where are you running off to in such a rush?"

"Billy," the teacher whispered, "what are you doing here?"

They stood holding hands in the cold night air. Sabrina rolled her eyes.

"We're not going to go through this whole lovey-dovey song and dance again, are we?" she cried. "We've got to get going."

"What's going on?" Charming asked. "Do you have an update on the killings?"

"Rumpelstiltskin and the Pied Piper have been tunneling under the school for months. They are looking for the weak spot in Baba Yaga's barrier so they can try to crack a hole in it and escape, and Granny, the sheriff, Mr. Canis, and Wendell are there now trying to stop them, but they don't know that Rumpelstiltskin is like a living battery with the power to explode, and if he does, he'll collapse the tunnel, and everyone inside will die," Daphne said, breathing heavily.

Charming stood still with wide eyes. "What was that again?" he asked.

"We're going to save the day," Ms. White said.

"We'll take my car," the mayor declared, leading the group to his stretch limousine. Mr. Seven got out of the driver's seat, but Charming held up his hand.

"Seven," he commanded, "we need to get to the school as fast as we can!"

The little man crawled back into his seat, closed the door, and started the engine. Once everyone was inside, he pulled into the road and sped off like a NASCAR driver, leaving tire rubber on the pavement behind him.

"You've done good work, Grimms," the mayor said as he reached into his pocket and took out a small box of matches, handing them to Sabrina. "We made a deal. Here's my end of the bargain. Let it never be said that I'm not a man of my word."

"Uh, thanks?" Sabrina said. "I'll save these for the next time I need to build a campfire."

"Child, those aren't ordinary matches!" Charming groaned. "They once belonged to the Little Match Girl. I just handed you something most people in this town would kill for."

Snow White gasped. "I heard a rumor they had been destroyed!"

"I was the one who spread it," Charming said. "If anyone knew these still existed, there would be chaos in the streets."

Sabrina peeked into the matchbox. Two small wooden matches lay inside. "What do they do?"

"I thought you two were supposed to be experts on fables

and fairy tales. 'The Little Match Girl' is one of Hans Christian Andersen's most famous accounts."

"You've been in our house. There are, like, a million books in the bathroom alone. We don't know everything yet," Sabrina said.

"The Little Match Girl sold matches in the street for money," Snow White explained. "One day she came across a box of them and set out to make a little money to help feed her family. But it was horribly cold outside, and she was forced to light one to keep herself warm. The flame became a magical portal, leading to a room filled with food and a roaring fireplace. The girl realized she had just wished she was in such a place, and when she struck the match the flames took her there. Sabrina, all you have to do is wish."

"Like Dorothy's slippers?" Daphne asked. She and her sister had used them to pop up all over town, but they'd lost one of them while running from a giant.

"These are more powerful than the slippers," Charming said. "They could take an Everafter to the other side of the barrier, or they could take you to your parents."

"Why would you do this for us?" Sabrina asked.

"We made a deal," Charming said.

Sabrina stared down into the box, and a tear rolled down her cheek. She didn't deserve such an amazing gift, and she knew it. For weeks she had looked at every Everafter as a suspect in her parents' kidnapping. She had turned everyone against her and practically broken her grandmother's heart. And yet, here was the most obnoxious, untrustworthy Everafter of the bunch, handing her the key to finding her parents.

"You could have used these to escape," said Sabrina.

"There was something that kept me here," Charming said, shooting a glance at Ms. White. She caught his eye and smiled, then leaned over and kissed him.

"Billy Charming, make me a promise," she said, taking him by the hand.

"What kind of promise?" Charming asked, somewhat breathless.

"When all this is said and done," Snow White said, "take me to the movies."

Charming grinned like a little boy. "I can't think of anything I'd rather do."

Mr. Seven turned and smiled. "It's about time."

"Eyes on the road, fool!" Charming shouted at him, but his tone had lost its usual bite.

"This is so romantic," Daphne blubbered. "I think I'm going to cry!"

"I think I'm going to lose my lunch," Puck groaned.

Suddenly, the car came to a screeching halt.

"Seven, why have we stopped?" Charming demanded.

"The road is blocked, sir," the little man said, pointing out the

window to where dozens of children were walking in the middle of the street. All of them were wearing pajamas. "There are too many of them to get around."

Mr. Seven honked the horn, but it had no effect on the children.

"The Piper is controlling them," Sabrina said as they passed some of the kids. Every one of them had a glassy look in their eyes.

"We'll walk from here," Charming said. They got out of the car, leaving Mr. Seven behind to guard it. The moment Puck was on his feet, his wings sprang from his back, and he fluttered into the air.

"What I wouldn't do for a carton of eggs," he said as he gazed down on all the zombie kids. "I'm going to get some."

Before he could fly away, Snow White grabbed his leg and yanked him back down to the ground. "We should stay together," she said. The boy looked extremely disappointed, but his wings disappeared nonetheless.

The group wove in and out of the crowd until they were standing on the front lawn of the elementary school. As they approached the main entrance, Sabrina noticed that the front doors the giant mouse had plowed through were still lying on the ground, and a steady stream of vacant-faced children shuffled through them and into the school. They were ushered in by a hulking girl with a pink ribbon in her hair. Sabrina recognized her immediately.

"Natalie, you need to get as far away from here as you can," she warned. "This place is going to get dangerous."

"Oh, it's going to get dangerous, all right," the big girl replied as her skin began to bubble and inflate. Hair shot from every pore, and two long fangs sprang upward from her bottom jaw. Her eyes turned a milky yellow, and a long, hound-dog tongue crept out of her mouth and licked her lips. Claws sprouted from her fingertips. "Daddy warned me you might show up."

She lashed out at the group, knocking Puck, Charming, Daphne, and Sabrina to the ground with one great swipe. Snow White just managed to step aside, avoiding Natalie's attack.

"Egad, I didn't think you could get any uglier," Puck said as he climbed back onto his feet.

"Snow, get behind me!" Charming shouted as he leaped to his feet. "I'll handle this brute."

"Billy," the teacher replied, "this is the twenty-first century. Women don't need the white-knight routine anymore. I can fight my own battles."

She planted her feet and raised her hands. When Natalie charged at her, she sent a hard jab and a right hook into the beastie's face. The monster screamed angrily and lunged again. This time, Snow White's foot came up and landed a hard blow to the monster's chest. Natalie tumbled to the ground but sprang back to her feet, clawing and scratching at the pretty teacher.

Ms. White blocked each blow with super-fast hands, until one of Natalie's punches actually connected and sent her painfully to the ground. Instinctively, Charming and Puck stepped forward, ready to take over the fight, but Snow White flashed them an angry look. They threw up their hands in surrender and moved aside.

Snow White sprang to her feet, planted them again, and eyed the monster with a smile.

"All right, Natalie," she said. "School is in session."

Natalie roared and leaped at her. Snow White stopped the attack by jumping into the air, spinning around, and roundhousing the monster in the face. One of Natalie's fangs broke off in the middle, and the monster fell to the ground, groaning in pain. The teacher stood over her with angry eyes and eager fists.

"If you're smart, you'll stay down," she said.

Sabrina and Daphne looked at each other in amazement.

"Snow, where did you learn to fight?" Charming asked, obviously stunned by what he had just seen.

"I've been studying for years. Now I teach a self-defense class for women and girls at the community center," Snow White replied. "We're called the Bad Apples. We meet every Saturday at four p.m."

"Sign me up," Daphne said.

At that moment the principal stepped out of the shadows. He was carrying a set of bagpipes and looked distraught.

"Piper!" said Charming.

"You have to stop them!" Natalie shouted at Mr. Hamelin.

"Natalie, this has gone too far!" Hamelin cried. "I'm going to let them save their grandmother and her friends. Once they're safe, we can finish our plans."

"No! Take care of them now, or I'll tell Daddy," Natalie threatened. "He's got your precious Wendell."

"We can help you get him back," Sabrina promised.

"No, you can't," Hamelin said as he raised his bagpipes' blowpipe to his mouth. "Rumpelstiltskin is too powerful. You can't beat him, and I can't take the risk. You have to understand. I'm sorry."

He took a deep breath and blew a long, sorrowful note into the air, and then everything went black.

10

"SABRINA! WAKE UP!" A VOICE SHOUTED FROM far away. She tried very hard to pay attention to it, but she was exhausted and dizzy. "Sabrina, you have to wake up now!"

She slowly opened her eyes. Mr. Hamelin was standing over her with a wild, desperate look on his face.

"What are you doing in my bedroom?" she grumbled.

"Sabrina, we're under the school!" Hamelin said, sounding frantic. "I know it's hard, but try to concentrate."

Sabrina looked around and saw she was standing in a huge tunnel, where children were rushing back and forth with wheelbarrows full of dirt and rubble. She looked down at herself and saw she was covered in soot and holding a shovel.

"Do you understand what has happened to you?" Hamelin asked.

"No," the girl replied. Her head felt so heavy, she could hardly keep it up.

"I entranced you and your friends," the principal explained. "I had to. They have Wendell, and they'll kill him if I don't do what they want."

"Where's my sister?" Sabrina demanded.

"They've got everyone—your sister, your grandmother, Canis, Charming, the sheriff, Snow, Puck, and my son—at the end of the tunnel. I managed to send you off into the mine to dig, and so far they haven't noticed."

"How long have I been down here?"

"Six hours."

"Six hours! They could all be dead!"

"This was the soonest I could get to you," Hamelin said. "They were watching me, but now that they've tunneled to the barrier, they don't seem to care that I ran off."

"Oh, I wouldn't say we don't care," a voice from behind them said.

Sabrina heard the sound of ripping flesh, and Hamelin fell to the ground. The frog-girl was behind him, holding a bloody knife.

"You're coming with me," she hissed, grabbing Sabrina roughly by the arm.

Sabrina swung her shovel and hit the frog-girl in the head so hard, the monster fell to the ground and moaned. Sabrina rushed to help Hamelin.

"Wendell . . ." Hamelin said as blood pooled beneath him. "You have to find him and get him out of here."

"I'll come back for you," Sabrina said, and then she ran into the nearest tunnel with her only weapon—the shovel—slung over her shoulder.

She scrambled forward, stumbled on jagged rocks, and accidentally kicked over some abandoned tools. Dust filled her lungs, choking her and making it that much harder to concentrate on where she was going. Each step was a challenge to her balance, and, unfortunately, her path was a complicated, twisting, turning maze. Every few yards, she would spot a child she recognized from school. Each was glassy-eyed, staggering through the tunnels, hauling buckets of broken stones. None of them seemed to notice her, even when she stopped and begged for directions. They were still under the Piper's spell.

At last she spotted a faint light in the distance. As she came closer to it, the tunnel widened dramatically, revealing an enormous room carved out of the Ferryport Landing bedrock. She paused at the mouth of the room, doing her best to calm her breathing and listen for any movement. Hearing nothing, she lifted the heavy shovel off her shoulder and entered, swinging the weapon in the air in case anyone was about to ambush her. But she was alone. Only a few old buckets and a couple of pickaxes littered the floor. There were no exits other than the way she'd come in. The room was a dead end.

She raced back the other way, passing more of the zombie-faced, filth-covered kids. *I should head in the direction they're coming from,* she realized.

She darted down the tunnel, fighting the crowds. At one point, Natalie and the frog-girl came lumbering down the tunnel after her, but Sabrina stepped into the line of children and, being as filthy as they were, went unseen by the monsters. The tunnels went on and on. Some led to massive rooms, while others narrowed so that there was hardly room for two children to stand side by side, but eventually she found what appeared to be the end of the dig.

The room was high and wide and filled with boxes of dynamite and mining tools. Flickering torches illuminated the room, but there were still deep shadows along the walls that Sabrina could not see into. Anyone could be hiding in them.

"I've come for my family!" she shouted into the cave. Her voice echoed off the stone and bounced around her ears.

An odd clicking and hissing sound followed, then a disturbing laugh.

Suddenly, something hit Sabrina squarely in the back. Unable to keep her footing, she tumbled over a sharp rock and fell hard onto her shoulder. Searing pain swam through her veins, followed by a dull, throbbing numbness. She tried to scramble to her feet, but her arm hung loosely at her side—it was broken. She cried out in frustration and pain.

Using her good arm, she picked up her shovel and swung it around, doing her best to make it seem as if she had not been seriously injured. She walked in small circles, scanning the room for the huge spider, but everything was so dark.

"I'm not going to be easy to kill," she threatened, hoping her voice sounded more confident to the monster than it did in her own ears.

"Kill you? Don't you understand? This is a party!" the voice replied. "And you're the guest of honor."

A long, spindly leg struck out from the shadows, narrowly missing her head. It slammed against the wall behind her, pulverizing stone into dust. Sabrina swung wildly at the hairy leg, sinking the shovel's sharp edge into the monster's flesh. The spider shrieked in agony. Its pain echoed through the cavern. In the dim light she could see its grotesque body flailing, then watched it fall to the ground. It knocked a torch off the wall, which bounced at her feet, illuminating the ceiling above her. There, suspended in mounds of thick, horrible webbing, were her family and friends. Daphne, Granny Relda, Puck, Mr. Canis, Snow White, Sheriff Hamstead, and Mayor Charming hung above, with only their heads free of the sticky threads. Their mouths were covered, as well, but Sabrina could hear Daphne's choked cries and Hamstead's angry groans. They were still alive.

The monster limped to its feet, then slowly ascended the

wall of the cavern until it was hanging upside down from the ceiling. Finally, Sabrina could see how gigantic it was and, more important, that it wasn't simply a giant spider. Its lower body was spiderlike, but its upper body had the chest, head, and arms of a boy. Even with the two huge pincers that jutted from his mouth and clicked excitedly, she recognized him as the annoying boy from her homeroom. It was Toby.

"Surprised?" Toby laughed.

"Not really," Sabrina taunted. "The bad guy is usually the ugly, giggling idiot."

"I've got a surprise for you," a voice said from behind her. Sabrina spun around and found Natalie standing there. Sabrina noticed her front tooth was now missing. Then someone else stepped out of the shadows, someone who made Sabrina's heart ache. It was her only potential friend in the entire school— Bella. The blond girl put her arm around Natalie's shoulders and smirked.

"You're one of them?" Sabrina asked sadly.

Suddenly, the girl jumped into the air, higher than any human being could possibly leap. Even more startling, Bella's hands and feet stuck to the roof of the cave, and her body started to change. Her skin looked as if it were filling with water. Dark spots rose to the surface on her hands and legs. Her eyes bugged out to disgusting proportions and moved to the top of her head. Her shoes exploded off her feet, revealing long, green webbed toes. Within seconds, she had transformed into the frog-girl that had attacked the Grimms. Like a streak of lighting, a long, slippery tongue shot out of her mouth, latched onto Sabrina's shovel, and yanked it out of her hand.

"Why did you pretend to be my friend?"

"Duh! I'm evil," Bella said.

The three mutated children burst into laughter.

"No, you're not!" Sabrina replied. "You're being manipulated by Rumpelstiltskin. He's toying with your emotions and making you do this terrible stuff."

"Like killing Mr. Grumpner?" Toby asked.

"And Charlie," Bella said, patting Natalie on the back.

"They just kept getting in the way of our father's plans," Natalie said as she transformed into the hairy animal she truly was.

"Your father? Is that what you call him?" Sabrina said. "He's insane, and when he cracks a hole in the barrier, these tunnels will flood and kill everyone in them. All the kids will die, including you!"

"Actually, the children are already outside, trying to figure out what happened to them," a new voice said. Mr. Sheepshank emerged from the shadows.

"Mr. Sheepshank!" Sabrina cried. "You have to get out of here. They're going to blow this place sky high!"

"Wow, Sabrina!" Toby the spider clicked. "You're even dumber than you seem in class."

"Hush, Toby," the counselor said, and then he turned to Sabrina just as he began to morph and bubble. Unlike the others, Sheepshank didn't get bigger. In fact, he got a lot smaller. When his transformation was complete, he was hardly three feet high. His head, back, and arms were covered in kinky brown hair, but his face and pointed ears were pink like a pig's. He had a short, stubby tail, hoofed feet, and a couple of rows of razor sharp teeth. "They're not going to do anything of the sort. I'm going to do it."

"You're Rumpelstiltskin!" she gasped.

"No fair. You guessed my name. Someone must have told you!" the little monster said sarcastically. "Really, child, I must agree with my son. You aren't as bright as your school records suggest. No matter. I have many names, and you were bound to guess one of them eventually. Just for the record, the one I like the best is Daddy."

Sheepshank extended his arms, and Natalie, Bella, and Toby rushed to stand by his side.

"Daddy? Daddies aren't sick perverts who steal children!" Sabrina shouted.

"I don't steal children, Sabrina," the little creature said, as if he was genuinely insulted. "I care for them. These children have been treated with nothing but love and affection. I give them everything they ever wanted."

"Then what do you get out of it?" Sabrina asked.

"Why, I get their love and their joy and their sadness and their frustration and their hope, and most of all I get their anger," Rumpelstiltskin cackled. "I get their feelings, child, every last delicious morsel of them. Their emotions are so raw and uncontrolled. You don't understand, do you? Let me spell it out for you: I feed on their feelings."

"That's where you get your power," Sabrina gasped, as Mr. Sheepshank's advice about feelings came flooding back to her. Of course he would encourage her to express her anger. He was eating it.

"You're starting to get it, Ms. Grimm. Children keep me alive. As people get older, they find ways to control their feelings, but not children. Children are like emotional all-you-can-eat buffets. So, where's a guy with tastes like mine going to find work? Why, Ferryport Landing Elementary, of course! And, trust me, Sabrina, it has been decadent. For years, I have sat back and feasted on the fights and humiliations you kids pile onto one another. The senseless bullying, the embarrassment of being picked last for baseball, the endless teasing about someone's hair or clothes—when it comes to being mean, kids are like master chefs, and I have enjoyed every bite.

"But there is a great big world of anger, war, and pain for me to feast on out there. So, when the Piper came to me with a plan to blow a hole in the barrier from below, I signed on. It wasn't easy, though. The Piper used his magic music, and every night the children of this school came to dig out the tunnels. At first, we tried to use all the kids, but the little ones are so weak, we had to make do with the fifth- and sixth-graders. Unfortunately, there was another unforeseen problem. The next morning, those same kids—the ones who supplied me with the most energy—were too sleepy to argue with one another. They went from a raging river of emotions to a dripping faucet overnight. I feared I wouldn't have the energy to do my part when we reached the barrier. But then you walked through the door."

"What do I have to do with it?" Sabrina asked, doing her best to buy time until she could come up with a plan.

"Sabrina, you're like the Niagara Falls of anger—it just keeps pouring over the edges. Every time you lost your temper, it was like a four-course meal with all the fixings. All of the paranoia and prejudice that run through you, all of the self-doubt, and, of course, the indignant rage about what has happened to you in your short life—well, it was delicious," Rumpelstiltskin said as blue electricity crackled out of his fingertips.

"Once I tapped into it, I turned up the volume on you and could barely keep up with the emotional energy," he continued. "Truth be told, we probably didn't have to kill Grumpner or the janitor, but I could sense how outraged you would get. And it worked! Thanks to you, I finally have what it takes to blast a hole in the barrier. Once it's open, I'll be free, and the Scarlet Hand will march across the world, destroying anyone who gets in their way."

"So you're the Scarlet Hand," Sabrina said, even now feeling the anger rise within her. "You took my parents!"

"The Scarlet Hand isn't a person, child. It's a movement, an idea. It's bigger than all of us. I am just one spoke in a very big wheel. Oh, I can feel your rage growing, Sabrina!"

"Where's my son?" Principal Hamelin shouted as he charged into the cave.

Surprised, Rumpelstiltskin shrieked and moved to safety behind Natalie's hulking body. The principal looked exhausted, beaten, and on the edge of madness. His shirt was covered with blood, and he limped painfully. In his hands were his bagpipes. "Tell me where my boy is, or I will play a song that will tear you apart."

"Wendell got in the way!" the tiny monster cried, gnashing his teeth at his much taller partner. "I warned you about keeping him under control."

He pointed to the ceiling. High on the cave wall, away from the others, was a mound of webbing from which no head poked and no movement came at all.

Hamelin fell to his knees and buried his head in his hands. "I've been a fool!"

"Bring him down, Toby," Rumpelstiltskin said.

"Awww, Dad. He was almost ready to eat," the spider boy whined.

"Go on, son," Rumpelstiltskin said.

Reluctantly, Toby scaled the wall, cut the web loose with his razor-sharp legs, and carried the boy gingerly to the ground. He set Wendell down at Hamelin's feet and scurried back to his father.

Hamelin tore the rest of the threads off his son. When the boy was finally free, he leaned down to listen for breathing.

Natalie rushed to a corner of the room and returned with a paint can. She dipped her hand inside it, and when she pulled it out, it was covered in red. "Should I place the mark on the kid's body?"

Hamelin shook with fury. "Stay away from him! All of you, just stay away! You and your Scarlet Hand, killing innocents. This wasn't part of our plan, troll! I just wanted out of this town so I could give my son a normal life."

"If we'd done it your way, we'd never have gotten this far. You've never had the backbone to do what needs to be done, Piper," the little creature said. "Someone had to make the hard decisions."

"Like killing my boy?" Hamelin said.

"I know your pain," Rumpelstiltskin said. "If I were to lose one of my children, I would be heartbroken, too. But sacrifices have to be made to please the Master."

"The who?" Sabrina cried, but no one answered her.

Hamelin set his boy down gently and climbed to his feet. He took his bagpipes and filled them with air.

"I'm putting a stop to this right now," he said, but before he could blow a single note, Bella leaped across the room, shot out her sticky tongue, and wrapped it around the bagpipes. She yanked the instrument out of the Piper's hands and into her mouth, swallowing it whole.

"That's Daddy's little girl!" Rumpelstiltskin cheered.

The monsters stalked Hamelin, backing him into a corner. Sabrina wanted to rush to his side, but Toby blocked her path.

"Without your pipes you are nothing, Hamelin," Rumpelstiltskin said. "And now that the barrier has been reached, your usefulness has expired."

"Leave him alone!" Sabrina demanded, but the monsters ignored her. The Pied Piper was about to die, and there was nothing she could do to fight the monsters off, but there was still something they didn't know.

"You're not his kids!" Sabrina shouted. "He played on the fears of your real parents. He made them feel hopeless, like they couldn't take care of you, because that's what he does. He plays with a person's feelings to make them do things they wouldn't normally do. He did it to me. I've said terrible things since I met him, things I don't truly feel or believe. He's done it to you your whole lives, but you can stop him right now. Your real parents have been looking for you ever since he took you from them. They want you back."

Toby looked confused. "Is that true?" the spider boy clicked. "You said my parents abandoned me in a park because I was a monster."

"They did, son," Rumpelstiltskin said.

"He's lying!" Sabrina cried. "I've talked to your parents myself. They didn't leave you in any park. Rumpelstiltskin manipulated your moms and dads and then paid them millions of dollars for you. He bought you, Toby, for the same reason that he bought Natalie and Bella—so he could feed on you! You're not his kids. You're his snacks."

"She's lying, children," Rumpelstiltskin said. "People are always lying about me! They want to take you away from me! It's not fair, children. Something has to be done to stop the people who hate me."

"We believe you, Dad," Bella said, her green face boiling with rage.

"Can we kill her now?" asked Natalie as she looked at Sabrina with murderous eyes.

Rumpelstiltskin grinned. "How could Daddy resist his little angels? Go have your fun."

"No!" Hamelin shouted. "This is going to stop now! I don't need my pipes to stop you." He reached into his pocket and pulled out something shiny, then looked down at it lovingly. It was Wendell's harmonica. He raised it to his lips and blew a low, sorrowful note.

Suddenly, a huge fissure opened in the ground. At first, nothing but steam belched out of it, but it was followed by a flood of ants, worms, roaches, centipedes, and a million other creepy-crawly things. They attacked Rumpelstiltskin and his "children." The frog-girl leaped onto the ceiling, trying to get away, but was immediately overcome by a swarm of flying cockroaches. Losing her balance, she fell painfully to the ground.

Natalie was quickly overrun with centipedes that wiggled and raced along her body, biting her fiercely. The monster girl growled and whined, but she soon fell to her knees, unable to fight.

Toby scurried around the cave, spraying webs at the sea of worms that poured over him, but the tide of insects was too much for him, and he was engulfed.

Rumpelstiltskin didn't fare much better. Leeches covered the little man, and he fell over in agony.

"Mr. Hamelin, please help me get to the ceiling," Sabrina said, grabbing her shovel. Hamelin blew into the harmonica again, and a rolling wave of spiders, maggots, and beetles lifted Sabrina high off the ground. Granny Relda was hanging closest, so Sabrina used her good arm to pull the cobwebs from the old woman's mouth and hands.

"Oh, *liebling*," Granny said. "This is one time I'm glad you didn't listen to my rules."

Sabrina smiled as she clumsily used her shovel to cut the sac of webs from the wall. The wave of bugs expanded to hold the old woman up, and she wrestled her way out of the sticky cocoon. When she was free, she reached into her handbag, took out a pair of scissors, and put them into Sabrina's good hand.

"These will make things a lot easier."

Sabrina rode the tide of creepy-crawlies to the next person, who happened to be Daphne. She yanked and pulled until the little girl was free, using the scissors to cut her off of the wall. Daphne was in tears, but she threw her arms around her older sister. The hug hurt Sabrina's injured arm, but she bit her lip and hugged back as fiercely as she could.

It was then that Sabrina noticed Rumpelstiltskin was emitting a blue energy that swirled around him. A fireball blasted out of his chest, sending a huge explosion ripping through the cave, incinerating the entire insect army. The wave of bugs that supported Sabrina, Daphne, and Granny Relda turned to ash, and the trio tumbled to the ground, jarring Sabrina's broken arm so painfully that the agony nearly knocked her unconscious. Through the haze of pain, she saw that the blast had damaged the foundation of the cave and that large chunks had begun to fall from the ceiling.

"Look what you have done!" Rumpelstiltskin shrieked. He

lunged at the principal and knocked him down. In the struggle, Hamelin's harmonica slipped from his hand and slid across the cave floor, where it was crushed by a falling boulder.

"Girls, we have to find a way to get the others down," Granny said.

"I have an idea," Daphne replied, snatching the scissors from her sister and shoving them into her pocket. She rushed over to the unconscious frog-girl, kneeled down, and rubbed her hands all over the beast's super-sticky skin. Then she rubbed her sneakers until they were covered in the goo. She ran to the wall, pressed her hands against the stone, and slowly but effortlessly climbed the wall. Each step made a squishy *slurp!*

"*Liebling*, do be careful!" Granny Relda cried.

"That is so punk rock!" Sabrina shouted.

When the little girl got to where Puck was trapped, she used the scissors to cut him free. Indignant as ever, he sprouted his wings and fluttered around the room.

"Someone is going to pay for this," he promised.

Meanwhile, Daphne went to work on Snow White, then Mayor Charming, and then Sheriff Hamstead, and finally crawled along the ceiling to the last of their group, Mr. Canis. But before she could cut away a single strand, she slipped and fell. Puck caught her just before she hit the ground.

"I ran out of sticky stuff," Daphne said.

In the meantime, Hamelin and Rumpelstiltskin were fighting ferociously, trading punches and kicks backed by hatred and rage. Hamelin picked up the tiny creature and threw him violently against a wall, where he slumped to the ground and lay still. Hamelin stalked over to him, snatched an ax off the ground, and, holding it high over his head, prepared to kill the creature that had taken his son's life.

"Piper, no!" Granny shouted.

"I can't let him live. He killed Wendell!" Hamelin cried.

"No, he didn't," Ms. White said. She was crouched over Wendell, holding his wrist in her hand. "He's got a pulse."

Hamelin dropped the ax and ran to his son's side.

"What do we do?"

Snow White laid Wendell flat on his back and tilted his head up. She peered into his mouth and then reached in and pulled something out with her fingers.

"He had some of the cobwebs in his throat," the teacher said. "He couldn't get any air."

She took a deep breath and blew it down the boy's throat. She tried three more times, shouting for Wendell to wake up, until finally he shuddered and coughed. He was alive!

Hamelin stroked and kissed Wendell on the forehead.

"Dad," the boy said, "I think I solved the mystery."

Hamelin laughed and sobbed at the same time. "I know you did, son! You're a great detective!

"Thank you! Thank you for saving my son!" the principal cried. He reached over and gave Snow White a huge kiss on the mouth. Charming was standing nearby and raised his eyebrows as Snow White blushed. Then he scowled.

Rumpelstiltskin staggered to his feet. He looked at his fallen children and sneered with disgust.

"It's over," Sabrina said.

"Oh, it's far from over," Rumpelstiltskin said. "All I need is a little more power, and there's someone in this room who can give me enough to blow this little town off the map."

Sabrina had never been as afraid of anything as she was of this little man. He knew her anger, he feasted on it, and she provided him with enough raw energy to destroy them all. But she wasn't going to let him play with her head any longer.

"You can't do it," she said. "I'm not angry anymore."

"I'm not talking about you, child. I'm talking about the Wolf."

Sabrina gazed up at the skinny old man still trapped in his web prison. Even from such a distance, she could see the fear in Mr. Canis's eyes. It was the first time she had ever seen the old man afraid of anything. It seemed to unsettle Charming, as well, because the prince stepped in front of Rumpelstiltskin with his fists clenched.

"We're trapped down here, troll," Charming said. "If you pull that stupid trick of yours on the Wolf, you'll let him out, and he'll kill us all."

"No, my friend, he will save us all," Rumpelstiltskin said. "The Wolf will bring the barrier down, freeing us from this prison! Freeing himself from his own prison, as well. Look at him—trapped inside Canis, parading around like he's human! It's pathetic. It's disgusting! We're Everafters. We shouldn't be acting like humans; we should be ruling them. The Wolf will be thrilled to help. His rage will open the barrier, and the Scarlet Hand will take the world for its own."

Mr. Canis struggled, but the change had already taken hold. The webs ripped as the old man's body tripled in size. A hideous roar echoed over the crumbling walls, and the Wolf was free. He fell to the ground, sending a shock wave through the floor as he landed on his feet. He looked around at the desperate group and licked his lips.

"Guess who's back?" he snarled as he struck Charming, throwing him against a wall. He sniffed the air. "Something smells good!"

Puck's wings sprang from his back, and he stepped in front of the Wolf. He drew his wooden sword and jammed it into the beast's belly.

"You take another step or try to harm anyone here, and you will have to answer to me," he said.

The Wolf studied the boy for a long moment, and then a chuckle came up through his throat. "Trickster," he said, sniffing the boy. "You have the disgusting smell of love on you. It will be your end."

"I didn't know dogs spoke in riddles."

The Wolf turned and eyed Sabrina. He chuckled again and then turned his eyes back to the boy.

"All right, lover boy. I'm going to make you famous," the Wolf growled.

The boy spun around on his feet and immediately transformed into an elephant. He snatched the Wolf up in his long trunk and smashed him against the wall. The Wolf fell to the floor, stunned.

"Fantastic!" Rumpelstiltskin cried out. A glimmer of blue energy began to swirl around him.

"Puck, stop!" Sabrina cried out, but Puck was too caught up in the fight. He couldn't know he was actually helping Rumpelstiltskin stoke the Wolf's rage.

"Stay down, dog!" the boy shouted as he transformed back into his normal self. He smacked the Wolf on the head with his sword and laughed. "Or there'll be no table scraps for you."

"You're a funny boy!" The Wolf sprang to his feet so quickly that Puck nearly fell backward. The boy's wings erupted from his back, and he flew into the air, hovering at the top of the cave. The Wolf leaped high, grabbing at the boy with his claws, missing him by inches.

Puck laughed and struck the beast's paws with his sword. If it hurt, the Wolf didn't seem to mind. His face was a combination of anger and amusement. Puck darted out of his grasp over and over again, until his wings clipped the ceiling and he fell to the ground. The beast lunged at the boy, grabbed him in his huge claws, and opened his jaws wide. His fangs glistened in the tunnel light.

Suddenly, Daphne was standing in front of him.

"Stop it right now!" she demanded.

The Wolf turned to look at the little girl. A blast of hot air blew out of his nostrils and into her face. "Don't worry, child. You'll get your turn to fight for your life."

"Daphne!" Granny called, but the little girl ignored her.

"Leave Puck alone," Daphne said. "And let me talk to Mr. Canis."

The Wolf snarled. "Child, Mr. Canis is not real. There is only me."

"That's a lie!" the little girl cried. If she was afraid, Sabrina couldn't see it. "Mr. Canis is real. He's part of my family, and I love him!"

Briefly, the Wolf's face changed. For a flickering moment, Sabrina saw his steel blue eyes change to Mr. Canis's dull gray ones. The old man was inside, trying to control himself.

"Child, you must run," the Wolf said quietly, dropping Puck.

"You have to fight him," Daphne insisted.

"He's too strong." A shudder ran through him, and any trace of their family friend was buried again. His disorientation gave Puck another opportunity to attack. The boy climbed to his feet and picked up a large rock from the ground. He tossed it as hard as he could, striking the beast in the head.

"Hey, Wolf, you ever hear of a game called dodgeball?" he asked.

"Death is moments away, and you want to play games?" The Wolf laughed.

Puck threw another rock, and it hit the Wolf in the chest, knocking the air out of the big brute.

"The rules are hilarious!" he shouted, bending over for another rock. With impossible speed, he tossed one after another at the beast.

"Puck! Stop!" Sabrina shouted.

The boy looked over at her. His face was red with excitement, but his eyes were full of confusion.

"Uh, I'm trying to save your life, Grimm," the boy said.

"You're going to kill us all," Sabrina said. "You're making Rumpelstiltskin stronger."

The Wolf staggered to his feet. "You should be a bit more worried about me, child."

"Take a look around you, Rover," Charming said, stepping between the Wolf and Sabrina. "Your little tantrum is helping to fuel your destruction."

The Wolf stood up tall to face the mayor, who continued, "The angrier you get, the stronger the real enemy becomes."

Ms. White joined Charming's side. She pointed at Rumpelstiltskin, who was encircled by his blue energy, enjoying each second of the fight.

"He's powering himself with your anger, and when he has enough, he's going to blow up this cave and bury everyone in it, including you," Granny Relda said.

"You're signing your own death certificate!" Hamstead added.

The Wolf turned to face the little creature, and immediately the blue glow around Rumpelstiltskin expanded.

"What are you up to, little man?" the beast growled.

"Your rage is exquisite," Rumpelstiltskin cried. "It's the best meal I've ever tasted."

"You're hungry for my anger?" the Wolf asked.

"It's fantastic," the creature said.

The Wolf eyed Sabrina closely. He had an odd expression on his face, filled with disgust and disbelief, one that seemed to say, *Can you believe this guy?* If Sabrina hadn't been so terrified, she might have laughed. The Wolf turned on Rumpelstiltskin and lunged forward, grabbing the little creature. As soon as they collided, both were enveloped in the blue energy.

"Child, you have to get us out of here!" Charming shouted at Sabrina. "You have to use one of the matches!"

Sabrina reached into her pocket and found the matchbox. Inside were the two matches.

"Sabrina, where did you get those?" Granny Relda asked.

"Charming. We need to get everyone out of here!" Sabrina shouted over the fighting. She removed one, wished she were somewhere safe, and struck the match. In the flame, she could see the outside of the school. Everywhere, dirty students milled around in confusion, having just broken free from the Piper's magic. She tossed the match on the floor, and a giant flame appeared.

"Everyone, through the portal!" Charming shouted.

Hamelin picked up his son and stepped through the portal. Daphne and Puck rushed to Toby, and together they dragged the big spider by his legs until they were all stepping through the magical flames. Puck raced back through, transformed into a gorilla, and hoisted Bella and Natalie onto his back. A moment later, they were disappearing, as well.

"That was terribly reckless," Charming said to Snow White as they took their turn.

"I believe the word is *brave*," Sheriff Hamstead said.

Snow White grinned and poked Charming in the side. "You could learn a thing or two from the sheriff."

Granny took Sabrina by the hand. "We have to go."

"We can't leave him down here!" Sabrina cried, as she watched the Wolf and Rumpelstiltskin fighting.

"I believe Mr. Canis knows what he is doing," Granny Relda said.

"This is my fault. I won't go," Sabrina insisted.

"No, child, you are not responsible for this," Granny tried to reassure her. When it didn't help, the old woman grabbed Sabrina's coat and dragged her through the portal. In a flash, they were standing outside in the cold, with a hundred elementary school students who were staring at the gorilla carrying a big, hairy girl and a frog monster.

"This is going to take a lot of forgetful dust!" Daphne said under her breath.

"Get away from the school!" Principal Hamelin shouted to the children, and they obeyed. They ran for the parking lot just as Sabrina heard a slow, horrible rumble from below. Everyone raced to the other side of the road, where some children were already congregated. When she reached them, Sabrina turned and watched the school. The horror unfolded like a car crash she couldn't stop watching. First, smoke billowed out of the school's windows, then a terrible explosion blew out the glass and knocked the doors off their hinges. The roof collapsed, a flame a hundred feet high shot out of the center, and then the ground sank as the school fell into it. Finally, a cloud of dust rose up, covering the site, and when it settled again, the school was gone. Only a huge hole remained as evidence that there had been anything there at all.

"It was my anger and my prejudice that did this," Sabrina said as she broke down in tears.

"Child, Rumpelstiltskin manipulated you," her grandmother insisted.

"He only manipulated what was already inside of me."

"There is a little ugliness in all of us, *liebling*. If it hadn't been you, it would have been someone else. You can't blame yourself."

Suddenly, Beauty and the Beast, the Frog Prince and his princess, and Miss Muffet and the spider raced through the crowd of children.

"We heard there was trouble at the school," the Beast grunted. "Have you found our kids?"

Puck pointed at the three unconscious monsters lying on the ground. The parents cried out in unison and rushed to their children. The Beast picked up his grotesque, unconscious daughter, Natalie, and lifted her into the air. "She's beautiful, darling!" he cried to his wife.

Sabrina watched the happiness in the parents' eyes. The Frog Prince and his wife kneeled down by their daughter, Bella, and slowly caressed her face. Even the spider cooed over his son, Toby. They loved their monstrous, murderous children.

Sabrina reached into her pocket and pulled out her box of matches. She opened it and took out the last of them. It would take her to her parents, no matter where they were. She couldn't be without them for another moment. She needed them right now. She made a wish, struck the match against the box's flinty surface, and watched the flame come to life. It shined in the cold night.

"Sabrina, no!" Granny Relda cried.

"Look at what I've become," the girl said sadly. "I need my mom and dad."

"Sabrina, you listen to me! I forbid it. It's too dangerous," Granny said, but Sabrina could already see her parents, safe and asleep on a bed, inside the flame. She tossed the match to the ground, and the portal grew. Without even a glance at her grandmother or sister, she stepped into it and found herself in a dark room. Her parents were lying on a filthy mattress, sound asleep, as a roaring fire kept them warm. She rushed to their sides, embracing each the best she could while avoiding her wounded arm.

"I'm going to take you home now," she said, doing her best to drag her unconscious mother from the bed and toward the portal. As she got closer she could see Granny, Daphne, and Puck on to the other side, waiting with worried faces.

Suddenly, Daphne grimaced in terror and started shouting, but Sabrina couldn't hear a word. Sound didn't cross the portal.

What is she trying to tell me?

"Did you bring my puppy?" a child's voice asked.

Sabrina turned and saw a figure step out of the shadows. She had known she might someday have to confront her parents' kidnapper, but her imagination had never prepared her for the person she now saw in front of her. It was a little girl, probably Daphne's age, wearing a red cloak and a twisted grin. Sabrina had never seen such an expression on a child's face. It was madness.

"Who are you?" Sabrina asked.

"No, you didn't bring him," the little girl said angrily. "But I smell him on you. Where is my puppy?"

The little girl reached out and put her hand on Sabrina's shirt. When she removed it, a bloodred stain remained—a handprint.

"I can't play house without my grandma and my puppy," the girl said.

"I don't know what you're talking about," Sabrina said, pulling away from the girl's grip.

"Yes, gibberish, that's what I speak," the little girl agreed. "Not a word makes sense. That's what they said. They said I had an overactive imagination."

"What do you want?"

"I want to play house!" The little girl's face grew very angry, and she pointed a finger at Sabrina.

"I have a mommy and a daddy and a baby brother and a kitty. Do you want to pet my kitty?"

Just then, Sabrina heard an inhuman voice slurping and slavering behind her. It said, "Jabberwocky, Jabberwocky, Jabberwocky"

over and over again. She turned to see what was making the noise, and a shriek flew out of her throat. Hunching over her was something too impossible to exist—a combination of skin and scales and jagged teeth. Even in a town like Ferryport Landing, Sabrina had never seen something so horrific.

"My, you are an ugly one," a voice said from across the room. The monster turned. Puck was standing next to the portal, hands on hips, like some kind of comic-book hero. "Come on, Grimm. I'm here to rescue you."

With a hiss, the portal burned out and closed behind him. Puck looked back and grimaced. "Uh-oh."

The little girl in red screamed with rage. "I don't need a sister or another brother! I need a grandma and a puppy!"

Suddenly, the monster swung its enormous arm at Sabrina, and everything went black.

ENJOY THIS
SNEAK PEEK FROM

THE SISTERS
GRIMM

~ THE PROBLEM CHILD ~

3

1

Five Days Earlier

SABRINA OPENED HER EYES AND SAW A MONSTER hunched over her. It was nearly fifteen feet tall, with scaly skin, two leathery black wings, and a massive serpentine tail that lashed back and forth. Its feet and hands were enormous, nearly as big as its body, and its head, at the end of a long, snakelike neck, was nothing but teeth—thousands of jagged fangs, gnashing in her face. A drop of saliva dripped from the creature's mouth and landed on her forehead. It was as hot as molten lava. "JABBERWOCKY!" the monster roared.

Too afraid to move, Sabrina closed her eyes and did the only thing she could. She prayed. *Please! Please! Please! Let this be a bad dream!*

After a few moments she slowly lifted one eyelid. Unfortunately, the monster was still there.

"Fudge," Sabrina whispered.

"Well, *good morning!*" a boy's voice called from somewhere in the room.

Sabrina knew its owner. "Puck?"

"Did we wake you? So sorry!"

"Could you get this thing off of me?" asked Sabrina.

"It's gonna cost you."

"What?"

"I figure if I'm going to have to save your butt every time you get into trouble, I might as well be paid for it. The going rate for this kind of job is seven million dollars," Puck said.

"Where am I going to get seven million dollars? I'm eleven years old!"

"And I want all your desserts for the next six months," Puck added.

The monster roared in Sabrina's face. A long purple tongue darted out of the beast's mouth and licked her face roughly.

"Fine!" Sabrina cried.

Puck leaped into the air, flipping like an Olympic gymnast, and clung to a dusty light fixture hanging from the ceiling above. Gathering momentum, he swung down feet-first into the monster's horrible face. The creature stumbled back and roared. Using its face as a springboard, the nimble boy flipped again and landed on his feet with his hands on his hips. He turned to Sabrina and winked, then pulled her to her feet. "Did you see that landing, Grimm? I want to make sure you get your money's worth."

Sabrina scowled. "How long was I unconscious?" she asked. Her head was still pounding from the smack the beast had given her when she stepped through the portal.

"Long enough for me to get old big-and-ugly here pretty angry," Puck said as the brute recovered and charged at the children at an impossible speed.

Two enormous wings popped out of Puck's back and flapped wildly. Before Sabrina knew it, he had snatched the back of her coat and was pulling her into the air, narrowly avoiding the beast's attack. The Jabberwocky crashed through the wall behind them.

"I've got the big one," Puck said as he set Sabrina back down on the floor. "You take the little one."

Sabrina followed his gaze. In the far corner of the room was a small child wearing a long red cloak that hung to her ankles. She sat on a dirty hospital cot next to the unconscious bodies of two adults, Henry and Veronica Grimm—Sabrina's parents!

How Sabrina had gotten into this particular situation was a long, and almost unbelievable, story. It had started a year and a half ago, when her mother and father mysteriously disappeared. The only clue the police found was a bloodred handprint pressed onto the dashboard of their abandoned car. With nothing else to go on and no next-of-kin to step in as guardians, Sabrina and her little sister, Daphne, were forced into foster care, where things went from bad to worse. The girls were bounced from one foster home to the next, each filled with certifiable lunatics who used the girls as maids, gardeners, and, once, a couple of amateur roofers. By the time their long-lost grandmother finally tracked them down, Sabrina didn't think she could ever trust anyone again. Granny Relda didn't make it easy, either. They hadn't been in the old woman's house ten minutes before she started telling incredible stories about the girls being the last living descendants of Jacob and Wilhelm Grimm, also known as the Brothers Grimm. Jacob and Wilhelm's book of fairy tales, she claimed, wasn't a collection of bedtime stories but the case files of their detective work investigating unusual crimes. Granny Relda claimed that their new hometown, Ferryport Landing, was filled to the brim with characters straight from fairy tales. They now called themselves "Everafters" and lived side by side with the normal inhabitants of the town, albeit in magical disguises to hide their true identities.

To Sabrina, Granny's stories sounded like the silly ravings of a woman who might have forgotten to get her prescriptions filled, but there was a dark side to her story, as well. These Everafters didn't just live in the town—they were trapped there. Jacob and Wilhelm had put a spell on the town to prevent the Everafters from leaving and waging war on humans. The spell could be broken only when the last member of the Grimm family died or abandoned the town. Sabrina warned her sister that the old woman's stories were nonsense, but when Relda was kidnapped by a two-hundred-foot-tall giant, Sabrina could no longer deny the truth. Luckily, the girls found a way to rescue their grandmother—and ever since, they had found themselves knee-deep in the family responsibility of being fairy-tale detectives, solving the town's weirdest crimes and going head-to-head with some of its most dangerous residents.

As they solved one mystery after another, the girls started to uncover a disturbing pattern. Every bad guy they faced was a member of a shadowy group known as the Scarlet Hand, whose mark was a bloodred handprint just like the one the police had found in Sabrina and Daphne's parents' car! Sabrina knew one day she would come face-to-face with the group's leader and her parents' kidnapper, and now, as she stared at the strange little girl in the red cloak, she was shocked. She'd never thought the person behind all her misery would be a child.

Sabrina clenched her fists, ready to fight her parents' captor, only to have a pain shoot through her left arm that nearly knocked her to the floor. It was broken. She shook off the agony and fixed her eyes once more on the child.

The little girl was no older than Daphne, but her face was that of a twisted, rage-filled adult, barely containing the insanity behind her eyes. Sabrina had seen a man with that expression on the news once. The police had arrested him for strangling five people.

"Get away from my parents," Sabrina demanded as she grabbed the little girl's cloak in her good hand.

"This is my mommy and daddy!" the little girl shrieked as she jerked away. "I have a baby brother and a kitty, too. When I get my grandma and my puppy, then we can all be a family and play house."

The girl raised her hand. It was covered in what Sabrina hoped was red paint. She turned and pressed it against the wall, leaving an all-too-familiar scarlet print. There were more just like it on the walls, floors, ceiling, and windows.

"I don't need a sister," the girl continued. "But you can stay and play with my kitty." She pointed at the monster, which was swatting at Puck with its enormous clawed hands. The fairy boy leaped out of the way, barely dodging the "kitty's" lightning-fast strikes. It whipped its tail at Puck, missed, then sent a filing cabinet careening across the room. The drawers swung open, and hundreds of yellowing documents spilled out.

"C'mon, ugly, you can do better than that!" Puck crowed just before the Jabberwocky caught him with its long tail and sent him flailing across the room. He crashed against a wall and tumbled to the floor but quickly sprang to his feet and snatched up the little wooden sword he kept in his belt. With a thrust he bonked the beast on the snout.

Sabrina turned back to the little girl.

"Who are you?" she asked.

"You don't want to play, do you?" the girl said as a frown cracked her face. She reached into her pocket and removed a small silver ring, slipped it onto her finger, and held out her hand. A crimson light engulfed her and Sabrina's sleeping parents. "Kitty, we need to find a new playhouse. Burn this one down."

The monster opened its enormous mouth, and a burst of flame shot out. The folding blinds on the dingy windows ignited, and flames crept up the walls, turning the weathered wallpaper to ash. The beast blasted another wall and then another, sending sparks and cinders in all directions. Within seconds the entire room was on fire.

"Who are you?" Sabrina screamed.

"Tell my grandma and my puppy that I'll see them soon. Then we can play," the demented child said in a singsong voice. The world seemed to stretch, as if someone were pulling on the corners of Sabrina's vision, and, in a blink, the strange child vanished into thin air, taking Sabrina's parents with her.

"*No!*" Sabrina cried, rushing to the empty bed as flames ate at the walls around her. It wasn't long before everything was devoured by fire and smoke. A terrible groan came from above, and a huge section of the ceiling collapsed right on top of the beast. The two children staggered back from the pile of smoldering debris. Puck grabbed Sabrina and dragged her toward an exit as parts of the ceiling rained down around them.

"I think this party is over," he said.

ABOUT THE AUTHOR

Michael Buckley is the *New York Times* bestselling author of the Sisters Grimm and NERDS series, *Kel Gilligan's Daredevil Stunt Show*, and the Undertow Trilogy. He has also written and developed television shows for many networks. Michael lives in Brooklyn, New York, with his wife, Alison; their son, Finn; and their dog, Friday.